THE PARROT

THE PARROT

BEN KOSTIVAL

Radial Books

Also by Ben Kostival:
Elm & North
The Canyons

Copyright © 2024 Ben Kostival
bckbooks.com
@BenKostival
All rights reserved.

Many thanks to my wife, my family, Tricia Yost, Matt McTammany, Steve Passiouras, Jim Nienhuis, Steven Moore, Neil Labute, and Patton Oswalt.

This book is a work of fiction. Any references to historical events, real locations, or real people are used fictitiously.

No part of this publication may be reproduced, distributed, or transmitted in any form or by any means, without the prior written permission of the publisher.

Published by Radial Books
radialbooks.org

The Parrot / Ben Kostival, 1st ed.

ISBN: 979-8-9907540-0-3

Cover art: *Parrot Snake*, Jim Nienhuis, 2022.
@nimbugallery

Typesetting services by BOOKOW.COM

For Hannah,
who accompanied me.

When he dreams, he dreams of violence. Kicking, punching, elbowing, biting. In a chunk of dreamtime—who can say how long in reality any episode lasts?—he runs through an encyclopedia of biff-boff-thoom-pow bodily assaults. Sometimes the victim. Sometimes the aggressor. Frustration dreams, he calls them, because when he wakes, frustration supersedes exhaustion as their most prominent lingering effect. Unknown cause or causes. Frustration suggests a thwarted advancement, a desire to move but for a blockage. Stasis, figuratively speaking. In his career. In his neighborhood. In his marriage. In his friendships, to which a special-status applies, a zero-status, for friendships and he no longer experience interchange. Once? Yes. College. Classes. Campus. Thereafter, career. The founding of his own business. Also, family. Wife and two kids in binary style. One male, one female. Time not in surplus for relationships beyond these domains. The relegation of friendships to tertiary standing. Inevitable, perhaps. Partly inevitable, to put the judgment on its firmest ground. In place of friends now, the people he says hello and goodbye to at the office when he chooses to work at the office, and the people from his bygone days who still receive his emails. His old friends now so physically remote that he feels he shouldn't count them as friends. Not in the normal usage. Barely sees them. Once every four years? Five? Can't hang with them regularly. "Doesn't matter. They're still your friends." His wife. "People mean their social circles when they say 'friends,' if they don't mean their online friends." Him. "Old friends are different. That's the point I'm making." "I agree. They're not my social circle. Acknowledge what that indicates." "But you can't say social circle either because then you're talking about social media, which we both know isn't your thing." "You're not kidding." "Don't worry about the label. Worry about who's to blame for the situation." "Me?" She raises her eyebrows. "Because I think it's more like it's no one's fault." Her eyes roll beneath her brows. The issue hinges on time. Consider its limited extent as it applies to human life. The dual natures of it. Of time, not of human life. Time, both generous and burglarious of gifts. Time, both creeping and of petrifying velocity. Vector entity rather than scalar. Freighted with quantity and direction. Quantity? Speed covers it. Direction? Forward. Which translates for humans into *toward death*. But, time's characteristics aside, the number of a man's days falls far short of infinite, and of *his* days, success and fatherhood have eaten their portions with gusto. The debate between him and his wife: an old one he doesn't want to continue. Conflict consumes too many of his nights already. The other nights? Blanks. Perhaps he dreams through them, perhaps not. He recalls only his fustigations. Imagine an injurious implement from fingernail to MIRV nuke and rest certain that he has wielded it against a contestant in his sleep or has had it wielded against him. In the morning, it bears repeating: frustration, exhaustion, spuddling. Daylight hours, send peace. Mercy. The quality of which does not strain. It droppeth, quoth the Bard, as the gentle rain from heaven upon the place beneath. Ideally upon his brain, upon his spirit. His again. Not those of the Bard, someone dead, and ergo, following Solon, happy. A relation that never made much sense to him. To the coder, not the Bard. The coder. His wife coined it back when she, then only his girlfriend, visited the house he rented with the other coders, his employees, for the marathon completion of his product. Triumphant, eventually. Sold for a boatload of gravy to a larger company. But through the years of the phalanstery, no emoluments. Everyone ate and slept minimally. Hygiene, an untimely consideration. To aid contemplation and to his future wife's abhorrence, he used to chew on his greasy, shoulder-length hair. "One day you're going to taste larvae if you keep doing that." Her. "I need the protein." Overcoming her disgust at the house's miasma of thought and software, she'd visit, confuse the names of the coders, call them coder one, coder two, and so on. His tag? *The* coder, with which he came to identify. "The coder tires." "The coder feels peckish." "The coder must sleep." "The coder grows fiery with rage!" His legal label lost out to a third-person joke. The state of affairs for so long that he sometimes doesn't answer when he hears his given name. And on mornings after a night of tumult, he often wishes to forget himself altogether. His eyes burn. His heart labors. His logy body drags behind his consciousness, which itself grinds only sedulously into cruising speed and altitude. In his throes, he thrashes and shouts. Triggered by fear? To suppose it explains nothing. Because fear of what? And springing from where? Again, not known. But known indubitably: asleep, he has dunted and kicked his wife. She has learned to scurry from bed at the first sign of an attack, yet both he and she sleep heavily. Unintentional consequence? Sporadic bruising of her musculature. Their long years together have taught her prioritization. First, escape the bed. Second, attempt to wake him. From his side, she chooses her moment. Shakes him. Hard. Normally sufficient. He crashes, crazy-eyed and gulping, into wakeful consciousness. Depending on the severity of the incident, the first thing he might witness upon waking? His wife at a wary distance, baseball bat in hand. Her prod for when his thrashing makes his perimeter too dangerous to enter. She needs a solid extension she can hold tight to and push on with some force. Thick, insistent, wooden, poking finger, the bat. Helps, too, for defense. Not that she has ever had to swing it to safeguard herself. "Give it time." His mordant joke. Provided she avoids injury, she suffers only the deleterious effects of occasional sleep deprivation. Bothersome, according to her, but no more than that. Jolts of adrenaline attendant on his explosive and unpredictable behavior, conditioned out of her by repeat exposure. After he wakes and acknowledges her with apologies, she lies down again while he, at the edge of the bed, collects himself and strips, as night terrors, enacted unconsciously for a blindsided audience of one, call down gouts of sweat. Into the laundry basket with his sodden shirt and pants. He clads himself again in sleepwear, throws a towel over his soaked imprint, and returns to bed, likely to the sound of the slow, purred oscillations of his wife's breath. She never rises to the volume of snoring. Comforting to him, her ability to fall asleep again. His sleep-tortures, not yet a nightly occurrence. Once a week, perhaps. Sometimes twice. He wishes for an all-out and everlasting surcease, dreads a gradual if not sudden uptick in frequency. Married to a lighter sleeper, he would find himself bunked in a separate room. And owing to the solid hardwood sound-blocking doors hung on each of the bedrooms, his disturbances do not rouse his children. They know of his troubles, sympathize, accept his thanks for their sympathies, and continue to string out their regular Zs. Eminently appropriate. Night terrors, his problem to chaffer with, secondarily his wife's, certainly not his children's. Yet all would demand drastic, remediate action in an apartment or even a house of closer quarters. Soundproof chambers for him to sleep in. Drugs for a near-coma insensateness. Contingencies so far avoided. Through a day-after, he struggles to recover. The orbits of his eyes feel caved in by punches. His body aches as from a trouncing. Self-inflicted. *And while asleep.* Injury and insult, proverbially linked. His body and mind, turned against each other, or both conjoined to turn against him. If he exists apart from them. However explained, multiple organs or biological processes barraging their host. Destructive parasites, the lot of them. The betrayal ganks his breath. Revisit the frustration hypothesis.

Renders sensible in many ways what otherwise presents itself as a riddle. All stases applied to humans produce the same result. He has thought on this. The somatic human must move. Posit even a soul, which, too, must move. From what to what? Darkness to light. Innocence to experience. Crescively, perhaps. Exactitude not germane to the question. The movement-requirement suffices. Basic middle-school biology. Foundational to the kingdom animalia? Motility, as opposed to sessility, which itself jargonizes stuck-in-place. Stasis births pathology. And he would not argue with stuck-in-place as a descriptor of his career and family-oriented lifeways. Cannot forget, all the same, the quality of his stasis. At a level of income most of his peers will never reach. In a long-married relationship he wouldn't dream of altering. With a freedom of schedule corresponding to Scandinavian welfare states and other utopias. When he wants to work from home, he can. When he wants to travel to the office, he does. When he feels like a day off, he takes one. When he feels like a *week* off, he takes one. Monthly quotas, his primary metrics. Awarded autonomy to meet them. Privileges afforded no one else in the company, which his intellectual property underlies. His innovations, his improvements, keep it competitive. *The* coder. Not that he lords his reputation. He has worked and continues to work hard. Except so what? Get stuck behind a garbage truck sometime. Watch the proles haul and lift and dump and throw their parcels about. Consider eight hours of the same. Consider twenty *years* of the same. Boggle that the human body can percolate under such sustained punishment and then tell yourself that people who earn infinitesimal fractions of your income *don't* work hard. For enough cash, people will accept any taradiddle as the truth. Not him. Knows luck's claim on his unparalleled position. Gratitude, always gratitude, the attitude he strives to maintain daily. *Hourly*. To not have to hack his way through Boston traffic every day? Miracle. Praise unto whomever. Home-based, he can take his kids to school, pick them up, fetch them should they need fetching for any reason midday. He forays to the office when his hours of solitude accumulate to intolerable levels, yet through mithridatism, his tolerance only increases. Solitude, kin to any other trial. Bearable after some acclimation. Time ago, he traveled to the office once or twice a week. Nowadays the same per month. "Too seldom." His wife. "No, about right." He feels less need for workplace companionship than he once did. His wife shakes her head. He sits with the silence. One cannot feel what one doesn't feel. His expertise? Demolition man. Software, what he daily obliterates. He sits before a facsimile of the network under contract. Probes for weaknesses. Finds them. Inserts munitions. Detonates. Crashes architectures. Explains to the clients how he went about sapping and how they can prevent others more nefarious from imitating him. Early days, overstuffed with face-to-face meetings. E-reports now chiefly suffice. Testament to the engineers and analysts below his pay grade on staff. More than competent interpreters of his analyses. In person, he discovered an all but unavoidable tendency to describe his activities in violent terms. He recalls an exchange. "How do you know when the architecture is sound?" The questioner. "When it's able to repel the bullets I fire at it." He regretted his choice of words, which that night induced dreams of mass shootings. Newtown rings as his mental echo to any suggestion of rampage. On the hideous day itself, he turned away from all headlines. Atmospheric human chatter would teach him far more than he ever wanted to know about this latest outbreak of American savagery. The facts confirmed the established features of his countrymen. That sickness afflicts them. That disease typifies their attitudes. That the national project rots at home and abroad. The fetor of a corpse-carpeted landscape. Firepower construed as manhood, bullets as sperm. Only a cancerous, gangrenous, leprous country responds to the mass-murder of schoolchildren *not* by doing nothing but by arming itself even more lavishly. Hooray! Next time, trot in *more* schoolchildren. We will murder them more massively. Despicable. And what of the murderer? Mentally ill. With-out question. Years earlier, *pegged as such*. Now consider his mother. Takes him to gun ranges. Because he enjoys them. Her mentally ill son gets his jollies from weapons and ammunition, so she sallies forth to subsidize his proclivities. Credulous American mindset par excellence. Schoolchildren, nothing but blood-filled balloons for unhinged losers to pop. Bottom-rung psychopaths. The gun-nut superpatriots, the worst of the lot. Pasty, no-account wastes of life burped from the slime only to sow devastation and die. Stereotypical American berserkers. Derivative because of their predecessors. Mediocre because of their Americanness. The coder can do what to stop them, redirect them, limit their capacity for mayhem? Nothing. The slaughter will continue. The slaughter will intensify. The ratcheting body count, effective advertising for perpetrators and orchestrators of perpetration. Vile. No other country would tolerate it. But here? Endorsed and celebrated. Protected. Goosed to flourish. America despises its children. Established fact. Look at the poverty. Look at the lead left to fester in the housepaints across the land. Insidious. Toxins migrate from the walls and sills to the younglings' tissues, from there to leach degradation. His countrymen make him ill and fearful. Survival mechanisms. But with numbers, he sands up the lizard-coinages of his adrenal system. Even working multiple Newtowns into the calculation, at-school remains astronomically the safest location for his children. Math education he does not lack. He understands statistics and can feel operating on a conscious level the paramount function of a developed intellect: to remove fear. The same reason religion hates education so. Likewise racists, xenophobes, bigots. Learning emasculates them all. Generally speaking. For one cannot ignore the German case. Rewind to the early years of the twentieth century. Germany, the most educated, most advanced nation, paragon of culture, unsurpassed in the natural sciences. The miracles of relativity and quantum mechanics, extractable in large part from German rigor and love of learning. Everyone knows what soon transpired. Unprecedented avarice for suicide and homicide. Concurrently. Twice in the span of a single generation. On the surface, refinement and cultivation. Scratch the patina. Barbarism. With such paroxysms, humanity advances. Germany, its pre-war culture exogenously eradicated, now one of the most decent countries on Earth. But the German exception excepted, in fear's absence, people must *think*. Explains why Americans love to cower. Because they detest thinking. The more fearful, the farther from thinking, the better they feel. The deeper into paranoia, the more extended their flights from thought. From rationality and reality. Not that any of his antagonists could articulate their prime directive. Luckily they pay him no attention. He tries to return the favor. Expatriate himself and his brood? He has examined the possibility. Has decided against it. Alone, only a puff of smoke would remain where he sits, with such rapidity would he exit the homeland. Enfamilied, he cannot inaugurate the hegira. Has first to consider how changing his position might affect the others in his life. His assets? Money, stability, a home in a desirable zip code. Twenty minutes, give or take, from downtown on the Blue Line. The ocean in his second-floor windows. Effectively seaside. Beachmont. The Mont, in family argot. Green months, he has to squint through a bracted and frondose scrim to spy pearl-topped blue waves, but in winter? Clear sight. Leaves dropped. Bare branches, no palisade. Grays and chalk-whites down the side of the Mont to the wrackline. Sun rising low and slow over the water, tinting a purple sky to cobalt and cyan. Winter mornings, he has to pull himself away from nature's display to begin work. Slippers, thickly fleeced with natural fibers. Flannel pajamas. Flannel robe. Knit hat. Kids already pointed toward classrooms. Wife already on the T. Ice-slicked Boston roads an irrelevance to him. Housebound and productive for the current rotation of the Earth. Mug in hand, coffee in mouth, eyes and face bathing in LCD rays. He scans the day's ration. Each module presents an ostensible hardness. He identifies a defect. Shapes a charge. Initiates. Rubble. Lucre flows in, commensurate with his dexterity. In this way, the years have raced by with even more breathtaking velocity than their one-twelfth divisions. Mid-career. Middle-aged. Stable. Durable. Powerless to control anything other than his own actions. Reactions, properly termed, since they so often occur in response to stimuli he also can't control. His generalized impotence distinguishes him from humanity at large? Hardly. Upholds his membership in the species. Considering all he has, he tries not to dwell on all he has not. Leads to peace in the night? Not a whit. Frustration dreams as ever. Daytime, when his brain unbinds from his work, he circles back, fugue-ing on common themes. Poverty. Disease. Empire. Entire regions of the world in flames. All alive can recite the litany, whistle the ostinato. What happens. What we can control. What we cannot. What we choose to stop. What we choose to continue. Actions pertaining to the aforementioned, not strongly coupled to individuals. In conversation, the brakes of his training—logic, math, operations research, to name three disciplines he had to subjugate—engage when absolutist arguments fly. The common observation, that individuals compose the polity. Granted. But one citizen within it? A grain of sand on a beach. A star in a galaxy. A galaxy lost in the Argus-eyed sky. Does not negate said individual's responsibility to behave morally. Simply extenuates his culpability if his polity transgresses. Makes of his contribution to the infraction a misstep so negligible that no moral machinery can detect it. Case in point, lead paint again. Suppose he opposes it, which he does. Suppose he contributes money to organizations that oppose it, which he does. Suppose he votes for politicians who oppose it, which he does. Now tally what he does *not* do. Volunteer his time to organizations. Comb politicians' funders for lead-paint hucksters among the contributors. Hound offenders with full-time activism. Credits, debits. Run them through the Babbage Engine. What he does minus what he doesn't. Result? A statistically insignificant wash. Morality cannot be divorced from efficacy. The ordinary individual, powerless and of no political consequence. And to those who try to disclaim the inarguable, the coder issues a command. "Stop thinking like a right-wing freshman." His favorite admonition. "Who's right-wing? I'm *left*-wing." The educated Bostonian in the outdraft of his ventilation. "Not if you think the individual matters. 'There is no society. There are only people and their families.' Pure Thatcherism." "Then, who's boss?" "The movement." "What movement?" "Exactly." "But what about me?" "What *about* you?" "What should *I* do?" "Be a good person." "I am." "Seems to me." "You're saying I'm not?" "I'm saying you are." "Okay, then what?" "Then nothing, politically speaking." "But what about what's going on out there?" "Out where?" "In the world." "It's going on, and it'll continue to go on. But it has nothing to do with you or me." "That's depressing." "Is it?" "To me. Not to you?" "It was once. Then I learned who I was." "Which is?" "Nobody, same as you." "I'm not nobody. You're not nobody." "We have a difference of opinion on this. But it doesn't mean we're not good people, because we are. Our friends and families are better off because of us. Yet beyond our circles, no one cares whether we live or die. Let's talk facts, not crap." His chit-chat with his officemates. He doesn't have cause to wonder about the mickle of leeway granted him to work from home. He proceeds on the assumption that when people talk, they don't just want to emit phaticisms from their oscula. He proceeds in error. Empty sound-making and meaningless badinage, the base aim of office interactions. He thinks of the advantages of deafness, of the appropriateness of simple hand gestures for upwards of ninety-eight percent of what qualifies as human communication. His contrariety unsettles the workplace. Stopping in here and there, all the office can withstand. Present every day, he would damage the environment. "Programmer extraordinaire. What do you expect? Good thing he's great at his job. Good thing he does his best work alone." Other people, encapsulating his traits. Stunning that a woman married him.

Doubly stunning that he reproduced. College acquaintances. Bonded over coding. Employed post-graduation, his wife came to enjoy the companionship of her colleagues. Blossomed among them. He didn't loathe workplace camaraderie. Nor did he warm to it. He opted for a different arrangement. Karmically positive, in its way. Since solitude doesn't bother him, better to work within it and spare others discomfort. "But it makes you nuts." His wife. "I feel fine." "Not that kind of nuts. The kind where the fact that you feel fine under conditions that would make anyone else nuts is the indication that you're nuts." "I'm nuts because I feel fine? How can that be right?" "I don't know. But after so much time alone?" She twirls her finger by her ear and swirls her eyes. He demurs, hardily, yet with qualification. He roves about, and not just with his wife. With offspring one and two also. Baseball games. Swim meets. Wrestling matches. School concerts. Salient feature of said activities, packed with other parents just like him. Parents with whom he tries to banter and small-talk. Goes over about as well in the wide world as it does at the office. "Your fine-ness. I don't buy it." His wife. "What's not to buy?" "Outwardly, nothing. Inside. That's where you've got a short." "You're in my heart now, dear heart?" "I've been inside it so long, I could draw its EKG." "I'm not uncomfortable among other people. Maybe I once was, but now I'm not." "Only a partial denial. Duly noted." He understands. She loves him. She wants him to feel present and connected. He does. Connected to her and the children. Connected also to the non-human biosphere and the universe of the inanimate. All in all, more connected than she to more entities, living and non-, than she. Connected to life. And enlivened by the connection. Sidling with minutiae equates to sidling with life. "I pay attention. That's a lot more than most people do these days. I lock in." His ability and willingness to investigate, she can't gainsay and doesn't try to, as she doesn't much disagree with his general self-assessment. She confesses more to a foreboding about the trendline, which she describes as a distinct and unmistakeable ogee toward shadows. "You're *off*, and getting off-er." "Evidence?" "All circumstantial at this point." "That's the case you're going to file?" "It's weak, I admit." "Short even of prima facie." "You're wrong. Anybody would side with me if they knew you like I do." "Where are these people? Trot them in. I have a right to cross-examine my accusers." "At the moment, I'm the only one." "I'm also entitled to the presumption of innocence." "So you are. That's why the soft indictment." "And don't forget about reasonable doubt." "I haven't surmounted it yet." "Not guilty." Nature, his refuge. When the weather cooperates. What nature a residential outlying area can provide. He likes to perambulate what he owns. Outside, his frontage to the street. Two patches of lawn flank the doorway and reach to the sidewalk. Along the verge of the house, a stairway slopes to the back yard, steeply pitched also, following the contour of the hillside property. Poured as a jut-out from the stairway landing, the shed for his garbage cans. Required of Mont residents. Rodent mitigation. Fifty-dollar amercements for violations. Lids on cans. Cans in sheds. Sheds shut tight but for collection days. The three rules Mont residents must obey lest sanitation workers mail back neon orange penalty envelopes filled with pics of unsecured rubbish. He ponders his cans and shed on a summer's afternoon. Warm weather. Software overthrown for the day. Sun fading. Air pleasant and humid with the sea's waftings. Heat without the buzz of noon's peak. Light falling. Opens shed. Opens cans. Deposits two bags. Closes cans, then shed. Ascends again to street level, re-enters house. Mixes gin-and-seltzer. Invites wife and family to join him outside through what remains of the afternoon. The closet holds lawn chairs aplenty. He removes one for himself, polls for accomplices. "The lanai allures." Him. "In a minute." "Maybe." "We'll see." His family. He knows he will sit alone, does not feel bereft. He has led his family to an option. Up to them to accept. On his stoop, he opens his lawn chair, closes the front door behind him. Sits down, fizzy tisane in hand, to watch the evening overtake the neighborhood and shroud it with night. Neighbors walk along. He nods, waves. Passersby pass by. Headed uphill from the T station or down to it. The T and the beach, the two most probable Mont destinations. Doesn't recognize any of the passersby. Consequently figures them for visitors. Nice place to visit, the Mont. Good for walking around. Beachmont, between the T and the sea. Lots of trees, lots of flowers, views of and breezes from the sea, depending. A day-trip from downtown to the Mont for a constitutional and a swim qualifies as a day excellently spent. He feels lucky to live ensconced already for the duration. Gives him a safe, relaxed fremitus. He drains his drink, puts the sweating glass down on the paving stones, tilts the lawn chair back and dozes. He wakes to evening and a scratching sound. Glances at the streetlamps, just beginning to glow. Summer. Streetlamps on means nine o'clock or thereabouts. Disbelieves he slept so long, then remembers: gin. No harm done, however, as he feels rested and owes no fealty to a normal schedule. Still and all, he can't stay on the stoop all night. He stands up, folds the lawn chair, wipes at his eyes. The scratching sound again. No, a tapping sound. Fully conscious as he hears it. Off to his left. Lower down. He looks from the stoop into the scaping, expects to see some animal gnawing or ferreting or burying or scarfing down a weaker lifeform. Dusk, the start-up of all nocturnal activities. But he spies no critter skullduggery. Now both a scratching *and* a tapping. From the stairwell. Who says humans can't echolocate? An explanation rises. The day's warmth. The garbage. Something has smelled it. Something wants it, wants into the shed. Not going to happen, varmint. The coder himself screwed the extra moldings to the seams, the metal flashings to where the plywood meets the slab. On the doors, latches that only human hands can open. Insects might gain access to the rotting trove within—he has yet to behold prognostic frass—but anything larger? Not a chance. Doesn't mean scavengers won't try. Vulture. Raccoon. Perhaps the coyotes ended their shaky self-segregation in the Belle Isle Marsh and now haunt the Mont's upper reaches, not just its base. The coder prefers anything, *anything* to a rat. Imagines a rat big enough to make the sounds that woke him. Shakes off willies. The bare, wormlike tails of rats horrify him into instant heebie-jeebies. Some people keep rats as pets. Rebarbative. Choose a beast and confront him with it, infect it with rabies first, if you like, and the coder will brave the situation so long as it bars rats. Yet as he leaves the porch, he steels himself for a giant rat because, really, one quails before the compassionless vagility of the genus rattus. Its conquest of the world so arrant, so total, its members plaguing the Earth in such densities, that any land-bound creature stands never more than ten feet away from a representative specimen. He rounds the corner, looks down the stairs. Gadzooks. Atop the shed. Not a rat. In fact, quite the opposite. A conundrum unlike those that sometimes bedevil him, problems at first glance moist and pliable but upon closer inspection protected by impregnable husks. Apply days and weeks of pressure with the high-speed drill of thought. Watch the diamond bit turn blue-white from friction and fail to mar the surface. Hope for an undermining, and hope in vain. The bit dulls, warms to its melting point, flows away. Along with it, confidence in mental puissance. Not the tiniest divot, not the pokiest cavity, does cogitation produce in the exterior enamel of the problem. Whenever he reaches this point, the coder folds to a type of defeat. He does not, however, surrender. He merely needs assistance to catalyze forward progress and bring his mind to fruitage. He and defeat pace slow circles about each other, holding eye contact at inviolable radii that tremble with unease. The coder must acknowledge his un-invincibility and at the same time subvert it. Dicey, this business of nodding to an enemy's existence, having to pay obeisance when tips of noses touch. Tactics can change, he reminds himself. Strategy cannot. He re-examines his approach. The acknowledging of existences, one thing. Granting them legitimacy, another. He does not truck with radicalism in that he refuses to accept subordination. The ultimate assessor? Him. Never the quandary at hand. How to shuck temporary weakness, regain deserved strength? The internet, which routs by instinct around censorship and damage, illuminates the janky path ahead. He shifts and bends, a branch-bound owl preparing an attack, sliding his perspective over and back, determining with his body the line of upcoming flight, which his eyes, fixed in their sockets, cannot divine on their own. Executed, the steps of a four-stage transmutation. Checkmate into check into stalemate into Potemkin facing. Yield! his inward cry. All defeat need do. And still it will not sue for peace. Armistice instead. Which the coder has previously negotiated. On this or that occasion. Diplomatic summits have punctuated the decades of his work. Longevity calls to equanimity for slow-release potency. He imagines himself not on the outside moving in, but rather already within and trying to seep out, his intelligence the dosage granulated through the insoluble matrix. Patience. With time, and by introjecting the effort of poppling water, he can turn the most impenetrable, japanned boundary into a sieve. Corollary, drive a nail not with the hand but with a hammer. Homo habilis, the tool-user, precedes homo sapiens, the thinker, for whom forward sometimes connotes a going back. From thinking to doing. From the mind to the hand. Equip yourself, worker. Enter the big boxes and examine the hardware, the miscellaneous saws, among which any neophyte can distinguish different types, and sort them into a crude taxonomy that can stand scrutiny under low levels of magnification. Now pupilize yourself to a carpenter and his pedagogy. Note how the designs of saws serve their duties. How designs nest within other designs. How the hand in stroking involutions registers qualities the eye disregards. In the fractal shapes of saws, a burgeoning nation. Understand the likelihood that your hands can only visit that nation, can reside within it only on temporary work visas. Fair enough. Each human life passes as all others have and will: subject to limitations.

Acceptable. And in most cases, immaterial, as few tasks require genius for completion. To paint the ceiling of the Sistine Chapel, the call goes out to Michelangelo. To paint the foyer of a hovel, Raphael will do, and not Raphael from Urbino. From East Boston. Who rides the T from Maverick to the Mont and who tows his supplies in a child's wagon converted with high rails to protect against spillage on day-jobs out and back. The hand, or hands, rather: supplementable. What the body lacks, the eye can see. Both work together to effect a physical grasping of the implement. Turn now to the mind, which tends to reject assistance, yet still can grasp. Reality stripped of actuality. Sometimes. Ideality unfogged by abstraction. On occasion. A basic poem. A haiku. Among the simplest. The poem achieves reality when? Upon conception? Upon mental composition? When spoken aloud? When written down? When read from a page? When declaimed from memory? Reality can materialize through so many spells that the magician doubts his own finesse. And the mind, beset by reality's disguises, moves its riverine essences along established channels. The Colorado never hops free of the Grand Canyon to choose an alternate drainage to the sea. The steep, high, stratified walls ensure that future flows resemble past ones. Portents of change, born only from a shaking of the Earth, a cracking of its surface, the uplift of one tectonic plate, the subduction of another. Catastrophic forces alone can disrupt patterns and overfly obstacles. The recruitment of catastrophe, though, depends on the depletion of surrogate techniques. All other avenues must first prove impassable before authorization clears for decimation. Stare at the obstruction, *think* at it, until the eyes bleed and the brain hemorrhages ischemically. Let the pressure build until, without deceit, you feel at ease that you have tried everything. The step beyond the final step beckons. Prepare. Accept the revelation of futility's arrival. Live from then on in the new world, the changed world, new and changed through conditions of extremity. The leap into the void must proceed from a stage, for the frustrated mind qualifies as a tragedy in the Nietzschean sense. The irresolvable conflict. Catharsis, the goal of the drama. The stage? For the coder, two options: indoors, outdoors. Only bachelorhood could save indoors as a prospect, and only then at the risk of forcing a permanent odor into all the materials of his home, for the molecule, the escape substance, the freebase mind-wrench, reeks of burning plastic when ignited. Injection, the scentless method barred to him by the difficulty of procuring the intravenous allotrope. He has tried the drinkable brew, the fortnight dregs of a witch's cauldron, but it tastes worse than the smoke. The brew's gagging savor, unavoidable, for normal gastric enzymes destroy the molecule on contact, necessitating the brew itself, which decommissions the enzymes. Not a gentle urging either, for the gut does not shunt willingly aside. Revolts, yet takes time to do so, the very time in which the molecule, having pierced the gut and entered the bloodstream, roams at will through the organism. For hours, as it happens. Hence the coder's secondary objection to the oral method: it takes too long. He needs to dialogue with the molecule for an allowable interval, not for most of a day. And when the gut reasserts itself over the power of the brew, hyperemesis commences. Projectile-style. Pre-position at close proximity a disposable, wide-mouth bucket to receive the cascading effluent. The more robust the brew, the longer the molecule's time of dominance, the more tract-rending the purgation. Meticulous chemists, those nameless rainforest shamans who originated the formula thousands of years before human writing appeared. With only primitive apparatus, mortars and pestles and contrivances that hack branches, they finalized their wizardry. Once, with a clutch of sub-coders in the time of his phalanstery, the coder set aside twenty-four hours for the start-to-finish oral experience of the molecule. Grouping up describes the norm. More enjoyable than solo. Groups, also safer because of the odds against every psychonaut dropping at once into medical crisis. The molecule has yet to cause a fatality, but whenever multiple people intoxicate themselves for hours on end in a single location, sober heads decide beforehand on a leader-director experienced in the trip. This shellback knows the currents, can help others navigate undertows and eddies, help not with a chart but with the taking of hands, the analgesic of skin-to-skin contact at sheerings, even though the territory never divulges itself twice in quite the same way. Safety first. The regnant OSHA commandment, as applicable in the purview of the molecule as in any workplace. Group-safety notwithstanding, the coder travels alone with the smokable form, a sticky orange grease smelling subtly of mothballs. He hadn't known the ancestry of his first dram, which came to him unrequested and unrequesting from a trustworthy vendor. Contemporaneous merchants would propound a vape, but brimming with what? Opaque fabrication presages adulteration. To obviate such, the coder long ago retained a craftsman adept at ad hoc synthesis and never transitioned to vapes. Held to the primal unction that baptized him and the paraphernalia thereof: the old wine bottle, label and capsule removed, thermally sanctified steel wool to imprison the dose in the bottle's neck, and the mouthpiece, a removable glass tube that seats in the drilled-through punt. In other words, the machine. The wisdom of his sacramental apanthropy? Shonky, yet redeemed by his expert renown. The coder thinks of himself as a skier who has slain the same chute a hundred times in conditions from slush to windpack to suncups. He does not feel in need of a guide. Prepares by crouching mindfully against anything apt to pounce. Panic, the archnemesis of inner- as well as outer-life safety. Chant soothing facts for prophylaxis. The ingrained knowledge of the molecule's transporting, hangover-less effects. Distilled water has sickened him more than the smoked molecule ever has. Attributable perhaps to its endogenousness. Introduced from without, the body snap-salutes it as a constituent part, metabolizes it just as quickly. Biology's particle-antiparticle creation-annihilation, a must of human evolution, as waking life could not proceed with the molecule at full activation in the body. Would result in long-term residence in the molecule's world—the dome—and would serve up experients to non-dome predators. Those of the real world, so called. Would march humans from peril to peril because for good or ill, humans live on Earth, not apart from it. They must take in all that surrounds them. An instantaneous debut and disappearance of the molecule, all the brain can naturally risk, despite craving this essential neurotransmitter. Craving evinced by active transport. Counter to evolutionary pressures, the brain expends energy to withhold the molecule momentarily from destruction. To what purpose? Science cannot at present say. The molecule, orphaned by research long before its listing as a schedule-one controlled substance. Illegal to possess, manufacture, sell, transport. Prohibition exacerbated its obscurity. Did not cause it. But did forestall concord. Banned, no one could study it nor discern acceptable uses nor scribe out margins of safety. What the coder can certify: that when in thrall to the molecule, the body falls away. He feels its departure and doesn't try to make it fast. Bless its departure and the ensuing lightness. Burdensome, the body. Don't pine for it. Perhaps his wife did. After her only flight, she stared clear-eyed, mute, and flabbergasted into his face. "Take a moment to re-acclimate. It doesn't lend itself easily to words, so don't feel bad if you can't describe it." Him. "How about, 'Not of this Earth.'" "That sounds right." "I thought I died." "You didn't, not pursuant to how we measure death, in any case." "But I'm here, yes?" "Of that, you can be certain." "Back from a weird-measured death?" "Maybe. All I know is, you *do* come back. If I thought there was any risk, I would have warned you off." "There's a risk all right." "I mean of death, conventionally understood. Did you use the trick? Did you let go?" "I don't see as I had a choice." "You did, not to stop what was going on, but not to resist it." "I didn't run toward it. I just stayed passive." "Good enough. It'll come to you. If you try to stand in its way, you'll just worsen what's going to happen." "What *is* that place?" "The dome. I wasn't sure if you reached it, but I'm glad you did."

"And the—" "Beings? They live there." "Who are they?" "My helpers. That's how I think of them." "And they *do* help you?" "Every time." "How?" "You were there. You know what they do. That's how they help me. Did you try to talk?" "I couldn't." "Couldn't try or couldn't succeed?" "Couldn't succeed." "How'd they react?" "They seemed flustered. I could feel how much they wanted me to succeed." "They go out of their minds when you do." "It was like they thought it was their fault I wasn't getting it. They seemed to be competing—" "To show you the best example." "Right." "Trying to one-up each other is their thing. However, I believe they're a consummate democracy, not an archon among them." "But what they do—" "Impossible?" "Yes." "Not for them. They do it society-wide. With a little practice, you'll be an old hand like me." "When I arrived, they were on me *fast.*" "Nothing escapes them. But don't worry. You'll learn. You'll blather a blue streak next time." "Forget it." "What?" "Never, ever, ever." "Why?" "Do you like dying? Because I do not." "That's part of the journey. The fact that you got there says you know how to handle it. You persevered." "A near-death experience isn't something I care to repeat." "Not near-death. Actual death, kind of. Because it's survivable. Weird-measured death, like you said. It's what death really feels like, except we get to come back." "I went once. I don't need to go again. Been there, done that. Next adventure, please. I can't believe you do it as often as you do." "Only eight or ten times a year. I barely even drink, which some people do every day." "What are you saying? You want to do it more?" "I'm just explaining why I don't think it's a problem. Leastways it's not addictive." "People become addicted to things for reasons other than chemistry." "Do you think I'm addicted?" "No, but I'm worried because now I know what it is." He later asked her what went wrong for her, asked her to itemize. She could not or would not, saying only, "Not for me, not for me." The expression of a preference put across with the vehemence of a command. The molecule welcomes those who come to it willingly, readies a different reception for those dragged into the hall. His wife embarked mid-ambit. Neither hostile nor enthusiastic. Prudent. Which sufficed to bait an adverse reaction, then precipitate it, then frighten her away. Too covetous of self. Perhaps her liability. The self, so precious? Laughable. Fasten rather to the numinous, the all, for the self mimics the body in expendability, the ego a loose fish not worth harrying. In reality, death wins, of course. The inexpungible fact that affirms the molecule's indispensability. The necessity of its rehearsal engine, its two-way simulacrum for the one-way trip of life. To the other side of human consciousness and farther still. Only then the abrupt turnabout and the straightaway regression. Traditional techniques of chanting and meditation, after decades-long apprenticeships of herculean difficulty, can unshackle perhaps a hundredth of the teleportative, reincarnative effects. Practice dying and rest at ease with it. Acquire the knowledge locked behind death's gates. To feel seized by death and yet know you still live, first-smoke's most addling enigma, with a welter to follow. The flight toward life and away from death. The abyss, something to dive into instead of shrink from. How then to navigate? By faith in the power of knowing over feeling. His wife's deficit. With practice, she might believe, but the fear attached to her first bobbling prevented her from trying again. Comprehensible. And for the same reason not. At times peradventure we cannot advance for lack of understanding. But to understand and *still* to stall? Unacceptable. Inhale thrice to create a ritual of the smoke. Sit for the flight or recline and where? In a setting that reinforces a serene mindset. Nature provides. The most common advice, of which he approves, for nature curls and loops and crinkles and rustles and sweeps and flows and corrades and moistens and generally complements life and the body. Nature minimizes the right angles of interior corners, the vertical lines of walls, the reflective surfaces of mirrors and windows. Harsh, sharp, and hazardous, the constructions of man. Minds careening among them risk incision and descent. But outside, the sky, tindering thoughts of liberation, presents itself for ready escapes. The densest, darkest thundercloud, nothing but vapor and potentials through which a mind can travel unimpeded. The coder, anchored by habituation, might infringe upon norms, but he can't alter the molecule's mephitic olfaction, an eye-watering sillage of sweaty feet roasting on a PVC fire. Needless insult to indoors, that acrid funk, and surprising from such an innocuous resting state. At room temperature, the appearance of earwax. But piped and put to the flame? Outdoors irrefutable to dilute and dispel the stench. The coder dons ratty, comfortable clothes for flight. Clothes fit for the incinerator, whether or not they end up burned. Dispenses with underwear. Flirting with overkill, he zips into lightweight, disposable coveralls, cinches the hood to scent-lock his hair. Properly attired, he can launch at will. Count down to liftoff. Rise under the full burn. Crest the stars and correlative inner spaces. Return to Earth. Strip naked. Ditch into flame or seal in a bag the chosen smocks. Shower. Scalding water. Strong soap with high lye content. Rough scrubbing, desirably with a stiff loofa. Plush towels. Crisp, dry clothes. Sound the all-clear. Unlike alcohol, the molecule does not perceptibly egress from the pores. Solitude? Nonnegotiable. His spouse and offspring don't need to watch. They would not understand what they see. He himself, the experient, barely understands. Coveralls recommend a launchpad somewhere on his property, not that a hazmat suit would necessarily draw attention. Two or three men garbed similarly for legitimate, blue-collar reasons ride the first Mont T every morning at five-fifteen. Another requirement, room to lie down. Smoke while supine. Don't court a toppling. Also, theorize a seizure. Look around. Remove what might contuse. Valid flight plans include the preemptive slaying of foreseeable dangers. No way to dispense with inside's strictures nor circumvent its deficiencies. He needed a four-season inside outside. His chosen castle-keep? The garbage shed. Within it, he pushes the cans against the closed doors and creates enough room to lie down on the slab. Upon the lintel, he stores a blanket to unroll for padding and insulation. He brooms the slab tidy, even mops it a time or two each summer, checks the cans for leakage and faulty lids. Solidity and tightnesses in profusion. The smell, ignorable, as garbage masks the exhaled, incendiated molecule. His sojourn, hours-long? Not at all. Minutes. Maybe ten for peak effects. But ten minutes relative to Earth, not relative to the molecule. Even after all these years, he struggles to describe its entheogenicity. Conscription of the elves? Gnomes? Beings? Creatures? Dome inhabitants? He has tested every category for suitability. None fit save one: gods. Hyperbole only to the uninitiated. Epopts might claim litotes. Which leads to the question of who or what supersedes gods. The coder does not know. Nor has he ever rested easy with the supernatural, toward which scientific education inculcates hostility. Spot-on, since antisupernaturality qualifies as science's raison d'être. Still, ancient guidance remains operative. By their fruits, ye shall know them. The evidence, mental. Therefore internal. Unobservable. Unreplicable. Unscientific. Except undeniable. The initiates *know*, albeit with the evidence of correspondence. Imagine two of them wrestling with mimesis. "Did you see—" "How could I not?" "And did they—" "As always." "And could you believe—" "I never can." "And yet it doesn't inhibit them." Allotted to every man, his internal state, and at the discretion of every man, to report on it. How many reports amount to evidence? To proof? Extraordinary claims require extraordinary evidence. The molecule as a conduit to divinities, an extrasuperextraordinary claim. The coder would like to *prove*. He can only regale, and a state of totalizing awe does not conduce with intellectual rigor. Power, what the molecule grants. Nothing, what it demands in return. Its nature, eleemosynary. No need to worry about hormesis nor the induction of tolerance. Minutes after the end of one trip, another can kick off, and with the same dosage. Ad infinitum. Hits as hard the hundredth time as the first. The recharge rate of its capacitance, almost as fast as its discharge. And the gods who upsurge, created or perennial? If the former, a hallucination. If the latter, the unveiling of a parallel reality. Either way, such generous beings. He vouchsafes to take and take from them what they give and give. They rush upon him at the bottoming-out of the third toke, which shatters the encompassing, kaleidoscopic mandalaverse of the second. The first toke, that noxious inhale, refines all edges, fluoresces all colors, brings close what lies at a distance and subjects it to high-acuity vetting. The light of Greece evokes congruent effects. An alchemy of sea, land, latitude, and atmosphere creates a clarification. The air and all its impurities remove themselves qua media through which the eyes descry the universe. Surroundings, in a vacuum and limelit by the fierce, undiffracted shine of a star. Astronauts enjoy the privilege. The only Earthbound analogues, citizens of Hellas and first-toke partakers of the molecule. The second toke wipes the familiar to the side, replaces it with a glistering chrysanthemum that pullulates beneath the familiar and subdues it. Then, toke three. An irruption and a breaking-through accompanied by sound. Cracklings as of static and crushed plastic, even of meat sputtering in a pan. Rapid, clairaudient vibrations hurtle him down a throat brocaded over all its walls with stipplings of flame and orange that shift and mutate and enflare themselves. His body and ego, lopped. What remains, transponding at incogitable speed, dissolving in the noosphere for the time of flight, crashing noiselessly through the chrysanthemum only to re-congeal. Where? Not specifiable except to say, with an apodictic semblance of subterraneality. The Earth's mantle might overhang the space that engulfs him, a sky-sized hypogeal curve by no means hewn from rock. The geodesic ultrastructure bespeaks machining from vanadium or glass, transmits a marmorated coldness that coruscates with iridescent shards. This rainbow epoxied on a chthonic cupola of lightyear radius? The dome. The commorancy of the beings. Upon his arrival, the coder conducts open reconnaissance, for of his presence he could make no secret. He has smashed through a revetment to stand bewildered in the midst of the indigenous, whose universe has unseated his. Lifted, the filter that screens standard consciousness from deviant, but every rendezvous proceeds with his faculties intact, for while the molecule foments a derangement of the senses, the most totipotent derangement man has yet substantiated, the senses operate normally within that derangement. No drunkenness, no physical destabilizations affect him. The dome, its bedizened tessellations twinkling with geometric mosaicisms, dazzles him on every visit, but rather as sensical, as not chimeric. Monumental and overpowering with the worked-ness of something actual, an edifice designed and built, yes with boggling effort, yes with recondite tools, but fashioned tangibly. In the gateway of the Loftollah mosque, for instance, the body, the mind, pause immobilized, but not for one second persuaded of extrinsicness. The transfixed marvels at how we, meaning humans, built this. Does not puzzle over who, meaning non-humans, pwned our ingenuity. Concerning the dome, built not by humans but built withal. Not the product of a fever-dream. The normality of the molecule's environs and effects, the way the emotions and intellect accept them as emitted along a known spectrum, the contradiction that greets him subsequent to the visual sonorisms of the chrysanthemum, the light-tunnel wherein composite radiations exert upon his body an irresistible pressure, delivering him in the perfect sense of that word, for he feels dropped off after a time of carriage, unloaded from the molecule's livery. Into the dome. Or beneath it. Contained by it, perhaps. Astonished by recognizable wonders. And among *them*, the gallimaufry by turns globigerous and discoidal, setose and cornute, filiform and geniculate, multicusped and palped. As they flit and deek in moire dermises of phototransducing opsins, the coder feels at their mercy, though they have yet to menace him with any threat more malevolent than an emanation of fantod from an echelon of backbenchers. Powerless. Without a doubt. He, the cynosure of their corybantic vitality, senses his utter enfeeblement vis-à-vis their talents. They receive him variously and always at speed, and even before he puts the machine to his lips, he anticipates this epibolizing enswarm-ment, which bizarre avionics facilitate. Girding himself, he thought-supplicates toward those who object to his presence. Acknowledges he does not belong. Cops to interruption. Pleads for all to make the best of his appearance. They never speak, this cenacle of displeased, but he can feel their exasperation as they conform to the majority and blend with his welcoming integration, for the gruntled far outnumber their opposites. The former launch into exultations. Huzzah! they mind-cry. You again! Just as we hoped! This in a language abounding from them in teeming philodendrons of *visible* grammar. Through passionate, synesthetic means bejeweled in all the colors of the visible spectrum, they demonstrate filigreed, ornate gossamers that glissade from solid to liquid and back again. Gleaming with facets cleaved by forgemaster crystalsmiths, these servings of language—dollops? pellucid prolate skerricks of dispersal? shimmeringly pristine driblets of pollutant-free glaciers?—erupt from the hands and mouths and fingertips of their bestowers, and the coder feels continually asked if he understands. He does not. His havering mind communicates such in turn, and perhaps because he has entered their world, they now feel at liberty to enter his, or more correctly, him, for as they locute, they bounce, exultant, into and out of him, throwing linguistifications that pinwheel away to form cities of malachite and jade, chalcanthite and amethyst. The bestowers, rapturous and rushed, ensorcel a childlike competition for his attention as they vie to surfeit him with mathesis. Look at me! No, look at me! No, me, me, me! They clamor into a gravid seriousness, a beseeching-ness, about the importance of their intercourse, no less joyous, no less harlequinized, as it imbues itself with encouragement akin to a demand. The coder's sense of the ambience? We love you and each other. Never doubt it for a second, and understand our love as rational. It explains why you must attend to our lessons. Do not crumple beneath stupefaction. Watch what we do. Absorb our instruction. Take it into yourself. Perform what you see. Don't wait! *DO IT ABSOLUTELY NOW!* His befuddlement, of no consequence as he gives in, floats within oceanic feelings of helplessness and powerlessness and spontaneously attempts the beings' artistry. No cities ensue, but rivers of language? Star-trails of the same? These he can generate. He has learned. Maybe just a single jot of the cosmic entelechy, but enough. And the beings celebrate his minor followings-through with a ludic frenzy of incongruous plainsong, chanting and bleating and jabbering as they hustle to flank each other and penetrate him. They titivate gifts a thousand times more ornate than any they've proffered before. Love envelopes him, love as the gaseous atmospheric component that he inhales and suspires and that sustains his life. Peaceful and womb-warm, this love, and he could go on forever, learning, practicing, exchanging enlightenments, refining his techniques, compounding all the wondrous deliria of the dome's ravishments, but only the universe itself goes on forever, as cyclic in modern physics as in Eastern philosophy, and so, when a tremor passes through the revelment, when the dome's spacetime integrants defer to a frisson, he tries to ignore the distortion. The beings note his dismay. They buttress him as the closing of the latest conjunction draws nigh. He feels a mild, outward riptide attracting the ghost of his solidity, the first stirrings of his impending ejection. The molecule cannot indefinitely withhold him. The prosaic grapples on and pulls, setting off wails and laments among the beings, saddened collective ecstasies of movement billowing with disconsolate goodbyes. The carnival must travel, must never remain long in the same locus, and he, who understands himself in this place as some sort of performer, must depart the stage. He acknowledges and mirrors his audience. Farewell. Until next time, which we must prolong. Tragedies, these short visits. We must not break away from such love. Enough to fill two universes and more. The riptide trebles in force, drags and tears at him. Disaggregation bristles through the fulgurating dome and its scintillating inhabitants. The coder longs to stay, but the shudder of elements, the bolstering, mind-space plaintings, denature him into a ration of quicksilver sucked at light speed through a wormhole. And he returns. To his garbage shed. To this world from the other. With his head clear. *And with the knowledge he needs.* How has he gained it? He evades the question by recalling the weaknesses, the incompletenesses of humans. Sometimes we know. Sometimes we can say. Sometimes we know and can't say. Sometimes we say and can't know. Unfeasible for him to Taylorize his knowledge-acquisition. His body, his mind, as begotten-of-the-primordial-ooze as any other living creature's. Only the molecule enables him to transmute bafflement into themes the beings can interrogate. The switching-on of a gene suggests itself as a homolog, a long-dormant phenotype attaining expression for the duration of the molecule's potency. His term in the dome, always just long enough. If he could linger, he might really come to know. How sages and seers know. Yet with never any surplus time, he undergoes his interactions. And awakens? Re-emits himself? Insinks dimensions? Crashes back? Into mundanity. The Mont. His neighborhood. His home. His garbage shed. His conscious body on the slab between the cans and the wall. He blinks. Perhaps cracks his neck. Sniffs. Garbage. No surprise there. Rises to a squat. Re-rolls his blanket. Stores it again above the lintel. Re-positions the cans. Exits and closes the shed. On with the day. Excelsior. Off into the hierarchy within which he labors until he feels the inclination to pull the ripcord on his savings and retire. His kind of freedom, unrelated to the billionaire freedoms of decadence, hebetude, affectlessness, childish libertarianism. The coder cherishes the obligations that ground him. For their sake and in curtsy to his wife's aversion, he courts discretion. He abstained during premarital cohabitation, but post-nuptials, inescapably, he reached a barricade he could only overtop with wings. The coder then proceeded, machine in hand, toward the outdoors. He paused in the room where his wife sat. The first occurrence in their married life of his unequivocal declaration to fly. She said nothing when she saw him. Returning, he expected a discussion. None eventuated. Neither on the second instigation. He relaxed. Steering wide of the subject, her apparent selected course. She accepted his priorities. Or signed an implicit truce with them. He left his thankfulness unvocalized. Better to reward her with sagacious use and eminent success. Also with love and offspring. All came to pass. The coder can look back and know that unless he manages to crack a tenth decade, more time lies behind him than ahead, and he arrived where he abides—financially, physically, emotionally, chronologically—in an attosecond. Yet he survived. Prospered. The peri-nightly thrashings of his sleep, he cannot explain. Gin and a lawn chair on his stoop can macerate him into slumber. Why can't his actual, material conditions? And further, why can't they gift him with the relief he feels upon identifying not a hyena-sized rat atop his garbage shed but the bona fide culprit? The stairwell glows from the streetlamp as exaggerated adjectives spate his mind. Effulgent. Outrageous. Magnificent. *Blazing! RESPLENDENT!* His eyes meet its eyes, or eye, because its head snaps to a new angle to inspect him monocularly and crookedly. The yellow-ringed black orb lances him. Bloodshooting the white, mid-face expanse: red stripes in crisp, finely penned lines. Pigment? Tiny feathers? Hemoglobin nitid through the walls of the vessels? The coder does not know. He resolves to investigate. The posture, the set of the head, the cast of the beak: quizzical. "Ooops, sorry." The coder, for he feels he has intruded. Then he laughs because intruded on what? A parrot. Laughter required. But he stifles himself because the feathers puff and resettle in response to an internal williwaw. The coder goes boulder-still for fear of triggering flight. His eyes begin to cool from evaporation, then burn from desiccation. He surrenders to the inevitable. Blinks. The parrot blinks, too, though its eye goes filmy instead of shuttering. Eldritch, nictitating eyelid. A stiffening then of demeanor. The bird looks away for many seconds before looking back again. Confident, almost haughty. The coder waits upon a parroty scoff that doesn't arrive. The bird's head moves up and down, scanning him. The red feathers above the eye stiffen and arch with skepticism. The coder feels in breach of protocol. But what breach? What protocol? The bird prinks the feathers on its breast, recovers a stillness. The coder comes down one step in the stairwell. The bird takes one hop back. Another forward step for the coder, another backward hop for the bird. Can't hop again. No more roof. The bird will have to fly. If it *can* fly. Injury or clipped wings might hamper it. Cruel, that clipping, or so he has heard. Difficult to know for sure, since Boston's definition of cruelty includes walking a bootie-less dog through five minutes of drizzle. Clipped wings tenably protective. Flightless and under house arrest, a bird can't fall ravin to a local manx or pitbull. Clipped wings could also militate against cages. Parrots belong in their natural habitats, but people *do* remove them. How best afterward to optimize housing and care? The coder can distract himself with that inquiry later. Now he must shove it aside and zero in. Parrot. Him. Their tense pas de deux, now paused. The frozen, non-linear situation can't continue forever. The coder onsets the phase-shift. He steps again. The bird loses patience with him. It flies off, alighting high on a branch in the backyard scrim of trees. Wings *not* clipped. Only to the edge of the boscage can light from the streetlamp reach, but the coder gains his destination below the perch. In response, the bird flaps once and gives itself over to the woods, dipping groundward before careering downhill, seaward, into the dark. Upon takeoff, the parrot flashes its dorsal side. Scarlet neck and deltoids. Beryl fanning to blue on the broad wings. Turquoise sparking down its version of a lower back and buttocks. Again a spear of scarlet edged with blue for the long, trailing tail. Bewitching. The coder looks away into the night, into the trees, streetlamp tickling the outermost leaves. Nothingness obtains except for the quietist brachial susurrus and creaking. The coder retreats inside, gathers his wife and offspring from their compartments. "Family, guess what happened to your father while he was outside." "Nothing." The others together. "Try again." "You sat down." His son. "You drank your drink." His daughter. "You fell asleep." His wife. "Correct, correct, correct, but *after* all that." Silence. "A parrot." He looks from face to face. "We need more." His wife. "I saw a parrot. It was on the garbage shed. I tried to get close, but it flew away, into the trees." "You're sure it was a parrot?" His daughter. "Absolutely." "What did it look like?" His son. "Like neon. Like light was shining out of it instead of onto it." "Light from where?" His wife. "The streetlamp." "Cool." His son, who walks away. "That's it?" Him. "We've all seen parrots before, Dad." His daughter, who follows her brother. His wife remains. Steadfast. Unrecreant. "You think it's still in the trees?" Her. "I don't know. I hope it's not hurt." "It can't be very hurt if it can fly. Did it say anything?" "Not that I heard." "Maybe it can't speak. Maybe it's never been trained." "Do they need to be trained? I assumed they just listened and imitated." "You should look into it." "Rest assured. Meantime, keep an eye out." "Good news is, it still has months to go before it'll have to worry about freezing. Whoever lost it will find it by then." "You think somebody lost it?" "If I saw a parrot around here, that's what I'd assume. Parrots aren't exactly native to the area." "True. I wonder what it's been eating, if anything." "Whatever it can find." "That can't be healthy." "You should research their natural diet." Even-tempered with a limit, her inquisitive disposition. So as not to rile her, he leaves her alone. Paces tight circles in the foyer. Entertains possibilities. Lost pet, the only explanation that washes. But it, like him, refuses to quiet upon lights-out for the house. He goes to bed. Can't sleep. Restrains himself from rising and jumping online to research parrot-centric texts. The glow of a screen in the dark supercharges insomnia. And already, his mind racing because of an aberrant bird. He tosses. Then sunlight limns the edges of the blackout curtains, gunning him into the day. He wakes his workstation, spends an hour ordering a half shelf of books. Same-day shipping. His hands sweat with anticipation. He can auscultate the internet with perspicacity, but to really amass knowledge, he eschews screens. This attitude from a coder? Sacrilege? Heresy? Hard-won understanding. Screens emit light, dodge invigilation. To squint his mind upon a problem, he turns away from artificial skies, a habit once widespread but now expectorating its phthisical death rale. For serious study: print, which reflects light and the knowledge it represents. For this position, he takes frequent flak from his wife, daughter, son, his go-to unwilling audience for all the abstruse information his brain accommodates. His family asks in permutations who designated him the arbiter. He knows what he knows because he opens books and hoovers their contents. His personality and history endow him with discipline and a long attention span, while his funds empower him to maximize both. Most people? Hamstrung from the start by sunup-to-wee-hours stints. Maintaining life. Supporting families. Fulfilling responsibilities. Securing necessities. The coder often mulls his apartness, wondering if it differs in any significant way from alienation. Books ordered, he cannot deny the force of a gathering mania. *A new topic.* An amphetamine-class stimulant. As his family awakens and trickles eye-rubbingly downstairs, his wife pecks him a wordless matinal greeting. In the front room, he sits with coffee and a book on do-it-yourself auto repair, trying to cover his anticipatory quivers. On her way to the kitchen, his wife stops and turns back to him. Not fooled. Leaves him alone to stew. His children see their father reading and drinking coffee. Inconsequential events. Wife to work, children to wherever children go in summer, he telecommutes, shuttling between his desk and the front window, overeager for his packages. Rips into the cardboard when the boxes arrive. Stacks the books and shreds downward from the top. Reads through the day and into a dreamless sleep at nightfall. Next morning, he collates breakfast for all in the kitchen. Burbles up coffee. Shirrs up some eggs. Whips up a batter. Scares up a pancake turner. Heats up a griddle. Family awakens. Descends. Wife and son, reliable attendees at the table when he cooks. Daughter less so, but sniffing hot butter and carbohydrates, she sits, waits as the coder trucks plates and a flagon of syrup from the cabinetry. His wife distributes utensils. His son extracts juice and milk from the fridge. The coder builds a Pisa of warm flapjacks, teeters it to the table. "The thing about parrots is—" "Here we go." His daughter. "We're in our pajamas. You're still in your socks. Give us a chance to wake up." His wife. "I'm that predictable?" "Old Faithful." His daughter. He goes into his study while they chew, returns with an armful of his cache. "And now, courtesy of the phrontistery." He drops a volume, lets it fall open to a dogeared page. Points. Gestures. Spiels. They humor him. They know how much he likes to pontificate. "You should have been a teacher." Inevitable comment from a mixed-company participant whenever he looses a payload. Cues him and his wife both, competing to see who rejoinders first, to denounce his instructional aptitude. Grading? Listening? Coddling for evaluations? The perilous navigation of intra-institutional political disputes? The holding of students' attention? Lilliputian, his chances of carrying off even one, save all, of these fundamentals, which teachers must prosecute daily. Expounder, more like. Disquisitioner. Adversary of eggcorns. Calquing, pleonastic virtuoso. Shameless strewer—with jactancy, parisological or not—of altisonant, recherché vocabulary plucked from continuous and wide-ranging reading. These roles he can apotheosize at home, where his audience, captive and inured to his pedagogy, concedes him minutes here, minutes there, the paterfamilias ipso facto owed a minimal dispensation. No school would stand for his praxis. Typically at breakfast, amid bowls of cereal, mugs of coffee, slices of toast, strips of bacon, he expatiates on his latest curriculum. Little excites him more than the fillip of the accidental. He had not suspected until the appearance of the parrot the fascinations it plighted. The coder, titillated, abandons himself to ravagement by curiosity. Van Gogh and Matisse, drunk on Mediterranean vibrancies, might have confected the birds that sing out from his books' covers and photos. Real, though, unquestionably real. These animals live. They thrive in the wild. Natural selection has selected for garish monstrosities. He indicates a specimen. "That's the one I saw." "That exact one?" His son. "A reasonable facsimile, my right honorable Weisenheimer." His daughter traces her finger to the genus and species in the caption. "Ara macao. Scarlet macaw." "Yes, and—" "It really is too early for this, Dad." His son. "He's right, Dad." His daughter. The coder looks to his wife. "Three against one." "I won't contest those numbers. Raincheck?" He takes their silence as assent and, book in hand, withdraws to his study. Closes the door. Perhaps his family has a point. Perhaps he has assimilated too much material too rapidly. He slows his breakneck submersion. Wards off hysterical blindness of the intellect. Turns his mental gears a number of revolutions. Worms closer the retractable hemispheres of his head. Attenuates the knowledge-monsoon to the showery patters of lowland rainforest where macaws flock, and not tribally. Species-mixers. Polyglot. Gregaristic. He imagines a ten-thousand-thumbnail array of profile pics, each beak ajar in an anthropomorphized smile. The word raucous attaches to the word macaw throughout the information. Anyone tenting beneath the canopy gets bombarded by fruit and leaves and nuts and branches. And forget about sleeping in. Parrot choruses rise with primate hootings to herald dawn. His parrot, silent and alone. Doubly anomalous. More evidence of a shut-in's escape. What resides of primativity in captive genes? Caged after the changeover of a thousand generations, the metal bars have to arouse keen thoughts of emancipation. But into what? Jailed presumably from the time of its hatching, the parrot must coalesce only vague inklings of freedom. Pushing toward somewhere else. Out there. Manumitted by unknown means, his macaw. Shocked at the freeness of freedom. Overwhelmed with loneliness, unthinkable in the jungle. The coder imagines tropical heat taffying his own muscles. Humidity dampens his skin. Beneath troops of monkeys and guilds of parrots, he tries to nap. Fails. The harriment from above prevents his eyes from closing. His imagination populates the canopy to mashing density. Monkeys languorous when not rowdy on branches. Eagles describing ellipses through smirred skies. The leaves as a-crawl with parrots as a metropolitan block with pigeons. The jungle: pongs of rot, wetness, manure, growing things, cavorting things. What green! Secondary color to the eye. Primary color to the nose. In his readings, new and delicious words tingle his palate. Phylogeny, the evolutionary development and diversification of a species. Basal clade, to which his macaw does not belong, the direction of the root of a phylogenic tree. Cere, the fleshy topping of the curved upper beak. Zygodactyl, two toes pointed forward, two pointed back. Powder down. Dyck texture. His breakfast soapboxing, discontinued at his family's behest, resumes after the interlude of the day. Take-out empanadas and pollo a la plancha from the Columbian restaurant at the foot of the Mont, the dinner substrate atop which he slathers terminology hot from his sources. "Is it worth studying so hard? In a day or two that parrot will fly home, or the owner will track it down, or one of the local cats will take care of it." His wife. "You're probably never going to see it again." His son. "For all we know, it's just feathers and bones somewhere now." His daughter. "Pessimists. You don't get that from me." "Don't look at me like it's *my* fault." His wife. "I'm not worried. The parrot I saw, no neighborhood cat could handle. It's too big. Its beak could crack stones. And if we've learned anything from the internet, we've learned that cats are scared of cucumbers, so they're sure not going to tangle with a decapitation gadget like that beak." "This is wonderful dinner conversation." His wife. "What about a fisher?" His son. "Do they live around here?" Him. "Definitely. We learned about them in school. My teacher is from Maine, and she said that up there, fishers are everywhere. In some places, people have to bring their pets in at night so they don't get eaten." "What *are* fishers?" His daughter. "I believe they're a kind of weasel." Him. "My teacher said fishers used to eat all the cats they could get their hands on. Paws on, I mean." His son. "Gross." His daughter. "A dead cat is gross, but a dead parrot isn't?" Him. "They both are. Meat is gross. I need to stop eating it. I'm gonna throw up the next time I bite into something and a vein comes snapping back." "Now *that's* gross." His wife. "I don't think anything smaller than a wolverine would have a chance against my bird." "I cry uncle on this topic. I want to hear about our children's day. Remember our children? They're the ones without feathers." He, not oblivious to his weakness for overindulgence, fakes attention to his children's reports. All going well. Bores and pleases him. Wishes for allied and favorable tedium to continue into their adulthood and beyond. His evaluation of his performance as an attentive father? Convincing yet workmanlike. Upcoming dinners, more opportunities for improvement. Until then, children to their pastimes and screens. Wife to some brought-home paperwork. He, prying with a toothpick at his gummy crevices, to his book-lined sangar. Cuckoos and swifts and hummingbirds, parrot relatives all, wheel about his pyretic skull. He learns the word for ninety-five percent of avian diversity. Neoaves. They sweep with parrots from the Cretaceous period across the boundary to the Tertiary. Sixty-five million years ago. The world-ending touchdown of the Chicxulub asteroid. The Yucatan bears the scar. Fallen-out iridium girdles the Earth for emphasis. Before, dinosaurs. After, none. Except birds. Only one and a half percent of the Earth's four-and-a-half-billion-year lifespan, those sixty-five million years. KT not CT, the parlance for the asteroid's before-after boundary. Fifty percent of the planet's species reached it, then stopped. Extinct. Mammals kept on. Parrots kept on, phylogenetically linked to songbirds after countless generations. "Parrots are monogamous." Him to his wife. "Some wrong ways are inter-species." Her. He teaches his daughter the word nectarivory, to subsist on nectar, and she, who has since renounced meat and adopted vegetarianism, gives him a thumbs-up. He tours megalandmasses. Pannotia, Rodinia, Nuna squoze together over time into Pangea. He treks the shores of superocean Panthalassa. Room enough in the lacunae of his cortex for these paleogeographies and more. Traverses Laurentia and Baltica. Seizes on Gondwana, where parrots evolved. The creeping divorce of the supercontinents draws itself out, with vicariance isolating populations and eons later kindling arguments among biologists. Cretaceous vs. Paleogene, the epoch in which parrots appeared? Eocene, as a matter of fact, the well-founded yet fractured opinion. From Gondwana, upon its breakup, to South America, Africa, Madagascar, parrots dispersed, colored shards exploded from the stained-glass window of life. Time, then as now, speeding and speeding, and even the coder, financially well-damped against accelerations and jostlings, must live up to his moniker. He brakes the onslaught of his reading to bulwark his salary and lagniappes. Codes near windows, scanning for the bird. Every weather- and schedule-tractable evening, he sips a drink outside until dark. Does not fall asleep in the lawn chair again. Perhaps should for replication. Can't. Watchfulness quickens him. Not cold yet, but in Boston, rigidifying temperatures lie always only weeks behind or ahead. When August's heat recapitulates July's by rising into the high nineties, the coder adds more ice to his drink and leans into the swelter. Far preferable to the nearing meat locker. He surveils, warier about approaching upon another sighting. His reading has schooled him on the incipient ferocity of the macaw. Wreaker of carnage, that voracious beak. Fruits, nuts, seeds, its regular victims. Fingers and flesh from time to time. Predation destructive enough to shame piranha. In screaming guilds, granivorous parrots will locust a tree to phloem, swallowing seeds and wasting, extravagantly, by discarding, with disdain, any extraneous pulp. Whatever infiltrates their u.v.-sensitive vision goes into the maw. Eggs. Insects. The sap of trees. Even their own kind, for they don't repudiate cannibalism. Parrots crawl through their brethren's burrows, ripping out throats, peeling the hides from breasts and backs to feast on the densest, protein-rich muscles. The upper beak, serrated, whets the lower in a continuous grinding, the soundtrack, some scientists argue, of a contented parrot at roost. But note the razoring itself, the thana-toid background music. Cannot ascribe benevolent intentions to the honing of a glitzing edge. And a parrot's shank, biologically affixed for indiscriminate use. Against naturally occurring poisons, parrots deploy geophagy, the eating of earth and clay. Buffers gastric pH. Counteracts toxic forage. Coats the gut lining. Shields the cells from damage. Neutralizes contamination via molecular binding. "If people could learn that, we could eat any plant we want." His daughter, with the zealotry of a convert, as he serves parrot-related trivia for pre-dinner hors d'oeuvres. "I know a kid who'd probably eat some dirt. I'll see if I can get him to." His son. "Don't." Him. "Your father is right." His wife. "But—" "Your mother and I repeat: do not do that." "Why not? I'd dare him. He'd do anything not to chicken out." "Maybe so, but we know nothing about local soil chemistry. It could be poisonous. If he ate it and got sick or died, that'd be on you." Him. "You're hanging with some real brain surgeons." His daughter to her brother. "You saw this thing once. Does it really warrant a major research project?" His wife to him later that night as they turn down their bed. "Just reading some books." "I know how you read." "Did you know that the pigments in parrots aren't found anywhere else in the animal kingdom? No one knows why. And there are different calls for different objects and activities. There's even a special call for getting airborne." "A pre-flight advisory." "And not only that, parrots copy the vocalizations of other species." "Like mockingbirds."

"I should check if mockingbirds can imitate bats, because parrots can. I find this more amazing than the fact that they can talk, which, really, when you think about it, is *nuts*. Their own language even has dialects. Members of one roost call one way, members of another, another. The dialects adhere to the roosts, just as in neighborhoods and cities. And where roosts border each other, the parrots go bilingual." "What if a new bird arrives?" "He picks up the dialect or he's out, unless he finds transplants who also can't speak it. In that case, he gets together with the other outsiders and joins their enclave." "What dialect does your parrot speak?" "He didn't say anything." "You're sure it's a he?" "Reversion to default. Sexing parrots is tough. They're monomorphic." "One-shaped?" "They look the same." "Then shouldn't it be equamorphic or homomorphic or isomorphic?" "I love it when you speak polysyllabically." "Just admit you don't know." "I'll bet it has to do with differences between Greek and Latin. I could read up on it if you want me to." "Please don't." "The upshot is, you have to do surgery or test their DNA to figure out male from female. Goes without saying that parrots themselves don't have any trouble." "The next time you see him, or she or it, ask how it self-identifies." "Around here, the spectrum is Berkeley-wide. I think it'll be friends with me once it gets to know me better." "Good luck with that." He strips the irony from her valediction and glides into September. Hot days, though the evenings reach with chilling hands toward October. The coder's consistency slackens. The nature of human patrols, to stutter. Yet when he can: on his porch, waiting, scanning, sipping his drink until the house reels him in for the night. Whereupon he can't sleep. The drinks and outdoor pacing exert no ameliorative effect on his insomnia. To summon repetition's talismanic power, in hopes the universe will hail his intent and sincerity, he raises each drink to the sky as it purples from pink to indigo to black. Ice cubes swirl and clink out a wordless incantation. He recalls the clothing he wore at the time of first brush, buys duplicates to safeguard a replicable costume, perhaps not attractive but not repulsive either, for the bird *did* loiter. T-shirt and cargo shorts, unsuitable outerwear in Northeastern autumn temperatures. Adscititious long johns. Wants later to stretch said shorts and t-shirt over proper pants and jacket. Wife vetoes the idea. "It's one thing to wear insulation, but you can't put shorts on top of pants or a t-shirt over your coat." "That sounds like a wager." "You might not care what our neighbors think of you, but I care what they think of me, and the last time I checked—" She waggles her banded finger at him. He obeys, and willingly. Not in error, this wife of his, for consider his recourse-gesture: superstition, vile superstition. The merest hindrance tumbled him backward into the headspace of an illiterate, landless peasant. His weakness lifts his gorge. And still he looks about. To the trees. To the understory. To the sky. To the wires. Copses. Roofs. Brambles. Transformers. Eaves. Bracken. Poles. Weems. Pigeons here. Chickadees there. The laughing, sallying gulls. Neighborhood residents all. No infusion of immigrant parrot energy. "Have you thought about going to the zoo? Whenever a song gets stuck in my head, I don't feel like I can clear it until I hear it again. Maybe seeing another parrot will cure your fixation." His wife. "But by your logic, I'd have to see *my* parrot again, not a different one." "True, but a zoo parrot might be your best shot at this point. If you call ahead, maybe you could get a zookeeper to put a parrot on your shoulder." "I always wanted to be a pirate." Slapdash, his responses. They amalgamate to contentless recitations that the etiology of his obsession outwits him. Cathexis because of benightedness. Cure the second to cure the first. Paradoxical, this bird, and as such, an embodiment of great science's fount. Not that the coder expects to discover quantum gravity in the plumage of a macaw. Rather, his captivation by paradoxes. Consistent with his training and accomplishments. The parrot, lively red flag, urging, taunting. The coder reminds himself that he cannot expect his feelings to exert fruitful pressure upon the universe. As the days and nights progress parrotlessly, the inflammation of his focus subsides to window-glances from within the house. His depressurized mental space makes way for its rightful tenants: family, work, gustation, secretion, conversation. And slumbration. Over a number of nights, he experiences uninterrupted sleep from pillow-impact to alarm-blast. Sleep that mimics inebriation despite his sobriety, which waxed as his vigils waned. He traces the palliation to hoarded and unrelieved exhaustion. An untremulous bridge across the autumnal equinox. October days then echo of summer, warm his grass for another coppicing. The last until spring, he assumes, though the shifting climate means he can't scry with conviction. Knock the liberal Brahmins for plenty, but for denialism about Earth's thermal throes, head to Branson, his synecdoche for the entire country beyond the major cities. Middle America. The land of incurious dopes. Whom bloodshed and witchcraft infatuate. But kudos to hereabouts. No quibbling on the relentless upward trajectory of average temperatures. Any unseasonably hot gust, tantamount to Earth's war-cry against its mortal traducer: humans. From the basement, he fetches his skifty electric yard-tamer, more weed-trimmer than mower, his property too small and steep for a ponderous gas-powered contraption or a ride-atop tractor. Preps himself ahead of time with a tepid, ceremonial stout. Pours it unwisely into an empty stomach. Giddy of head and balance, he plugs the mower into the outlet on the exterior wall. Starts the engine, which vibrates and whirrs rather than shudders and roars. Pushes off, and the grass, whipped low, sends notes of scalped chlorophyll, maple, and birch into his nostrils. Brown and red and yellow leaves garnish the lawn. Decoration for winter's arrival. Soon perhaps a frosting of white, but as he mows, clemency prevails. The breeze whirls a digestif of cold saltwater from the shore. He pauses. Inhales and holds. Drinks deep of all airborne draughts. Closes his eyes. Relishes, his chest expansive. Exhales. Bliss. His eyelids lift and readmit the world. *Which includes the parrot!* At the frontier of his

property. Perched on a stump that only an instant earlier stood unoc-
cupied. The surety of this fact grips him. One moment: depauperate
space. The next, in a reverse fulmination of flashpaper: parrot. The
arrival of luminous color against an arid, depleted background? Not
something he could have missed. But he did. And now he does. not.
move. Continues even to secure the dead-man's bar against the top
of the mower's handle. Release the bar, halt the engine. Any jar to the
ambient sound, the parrot might interpret as a tocsin and flee. The
coder watches, watches. The parrot regards him. The beak, slightly
open, closes. Opens again. Repeats. Repeats again. The coder feels
shoved by a realization. The parrot: speaking. Inaudible because of
the mower. Have to risk the risk. He releases the dead-man's bar.
Squelches the engine. Sudden decrescendo. Uphill, a car passes on
the street. In the brush and trees, the intermittent cheeping of chickadees. The parrot remains on the stump. No more beak-motion.
Only the resettling of this or that feather. "Don't be afraid. Go ahead.
I can hear you." The coder in his soothingest tones. The beak remains
closed. The head turns this way, trains an eye on him, turns the other
way, trains the other eye. Tinning from a catchpenny radio somewhere nearby: the deathless horrendousness of classic rock, which
the coder hates above all other music except country, the accom-
paniment to American stupidity. To launder these genres from the
phonosphere, the coder would bend the knee to any dictatorship.
He gutturals his revulsion—can't stop himself—and inadvertently
rowels the parrot. With flapping reds, it luffs the air and escapes.
The downhill trees obscure it again. The coder clutches his head. His
molars grind. He bustles into the house. "It's back! I saw it!" Him, to
no one in particular. "Saw what?" His son, from the TV room adjacent. The coder hurries in. Muted, the TV squinches silently at the
unsiblinged boy hurkle-durkle on the couch and intent on his tablet.
"Two screens?" The coder. "I alternate." "On what cycle?" "One or
two minutes." "Admirable attention span." "Longer than most of my

classmates." "I don't doubt it." "Concentrating is like going outside: not something kids do anymore." "Too bad, because you'll want to know what I just saw—outside, I might add." "The parrot?" "Yep." "Seriously?" The boy lowers his tablet. "Would I lie about that?" "Where did you see it?" "Out back on a stump." "What was it doing?" "Waiting and talking." "What did it say?" "I don't know. I couldn't hear it. I had the mower on." "Why didn't you turn it off?" "I did, but by then I'd missed out on hearing." "How do you know it was saying something?" "I could see its lips moving." "Beak." "Right. Beak." "Maybe it was just chewing." "No, it was talking. If you'd seen it, you'd agree." "Did you get a picture?" "Sorry, no." "This is why your rule stinks, Dad. If you'd had your phone, you could have gotten a picture. Pics, or it didn't happen. Everybody knows that." More a guideline than a rule, his predilection for traveling phoneless when he can. Not many opportunities to do so, but around the house? Wife and children accounted for? No better zone for an unplugging. He has preached to his children about the halcyon first decade of the web. Post-internet, pre-smartphone. Available, all the world's informational desiderata, yet subject to the restriction that you had to sit still to access it. At a desk or a table. Away from a terminal? Normal human interactions. Then, the early infrastructure's neutron-bomb escalation: the smartphone, which left intact a framework of humanity pasteurized of inner life. "What's my constant advice to you and your sister?" "Touch grass." "Okay, so, that's what I was doing, almost literally." "But look what happened." "The parrot came back." "Says you." "Believe your father, first-born son. He is ordinary in every way except for anything to do with tech. He doesn't know why he gets along with it so well, but he knows to mistrust the rapport." "How come?" "Because when you tune in to machines, you tune out to people. Try talking to somebody who's holding a smartphone. Can't be done. The instant it blinks or beeps or jumps, people disappear into their screens." "Phubbing." "We need a better word for it than that." "Talking is overrated." His daughter, who with his wife has entered the room. "Cyborgs." Him to his children. "That's what we all are now, your mother and I included." "Cyborgs have their tech grafted in." His son. "Cyborgish, then, assuming grafting isn't the same as never putting something down." His wife, very quick. "I put my phone down whenever I want." His son. "You put it down because we make you put it down." Him. "And cyborgish is bad enough." His wife. Tongue-in-cheek to some degree, his and his wife's criticisms. Their children behave in non-Aspergery ways. On family trips to the beach, every phone gets left at the house. Worst case, someone runs a few blocks home to address an emergency or asks a lounger on the next towel to make a call. The coder does enjoy his summertime excursions. Broad Sound no hot tub, though. Countable on one hand, the September days when the water achieves seventy Fahrenheit. Sixty, the July-August norm. Limits him to five minutes of immersion. And fifty, the coldest water he has ever swum. Plunged in for eight or nine strokes, then out again. More than that, he couldn't bear. But shoreside in and of itself tenders macrocosmic gifts. Shocking, the number of beachgoing hands and eyes tractor-beamed to phones. Over the majesty of the ocean, the tactile and defoliating pleasures of anhydrous sand, the scent of brine, the cries of gulls, most people prefer screens. Not his children. They know by instinct or reasoning that the beach, where the body achieves its most thorough christening in the elements, opposes technology. Engineering: anti-organic. Neither life nor lifelike. Who better-poised to testify than the coder? His tales of pre-cyborg times might resonate in juvenile ears as an old's shopworn whingings, but his children know not to misjudge him as a nostalgist. Pernicious drug, sentimentality. Down with pessimism and optimism and its hyperbolic American variant, Pollyannaism. The sciences, his guiding faith. Observe the facts. The world: visible, accessible, veritably haptic today. Years ago? Little choice but to know only your hometown. Assume its encirclement by voids where monsters dwell. Now we see clear to more hospitable terrain and can colonize it, so the coder retreats to his den, begins searching for the parrot. Re-checks online for lost-pet notices. "Nada." Him to nobody when he turns up zilch, but the Spanish word tweaks him to search bilingually, as Boston operates as much in Español as in Ingles. ¿Por lo tanto, por qué no buscar en Español? He enters 'papagayo.' And sure enough. He shouts to the house. "I told you I saw it! Come and see! Ven aquí!" The brood gathers around his terminal, whereon he expands an ad to full-screen width. '¡Se busca! Recompensa: U.S. Dos Mil Dolares. ¿Has visto este pájaro?' He clicks through to a website, meets a bird dominantly yellow with green rear dorsal feathers and an orange head. "This is your bird? Seems like it should be bigger." His wife. The coder leans closer to the screen, feels the subdermal heat of the monitor, hears the electronic thrumming of its neurons. "And redder." His wife again. His fervor has trampled his faculties of discrimination. In a sigh, the proper power ratio re-asserts itself. "Family, I am sorry to report." "That's all right, Dad." His daughter. "Better luck next time, Tiger." His son. "Do you still love me?" Him to his wife as she kisses him on the top of the head and follows the kids out of the room, waving backwardly over her shoulder. His embarrassment expands. How, even for an instant, did he mistake this runt for his bird? Wrong size only tops the census of mismatches. He also doesn't see in the photo the red of a lithium flame. Can the promise of two thousand dollars have briefly refracted his judgment? Vestigial of his no-money days in the rented coder-house? Too far back. Too much surplus bullion earned and conserved in the interim. He blanks the monitor. Pushes away from the desktop. Crosses his arms. Seesaws from tilted-back to straight-up in his chair. Scans desultorily his shelves of books. The room where he sits: the central monument to his lifetime of short-duration fetishes and lucubrations. Here, his books on modern art. There, his books on land management. Abutting the stacks, the wooden chest jumbled with books on bread-making. Elsewhere, his run of materials on the early history of computers. No tsundoku for him. What he buys, he reads. Just to say he'd done it, he once read the Bible from page one to the end. Proust also. Fifty pages a day for two and a half months. Now he has crammed horizontally above those spines his parrot research. He gets up to examine the trove. At the shelf, he stands with his hands in his pockets, not reaching for a volume. Chockablock, these books. He masoned them himself upon their completions. He remembers previous idées fixe, how lifeless they felt. Whereas the parrot, animate, interactive, wants to consociate. The coder can't unsee what he saw. The moving beak, articulating. What information? The fugitive answer needles him. He cannot cave. He must act. Construct an attractive experiment. Across a swath of books, a shadow flits through a stave of sunlight. He turns too late to glimpse the source, yet in his turning perceives afresh the light and shadow and gateway. Moron. Should have done it after sighting-zero. Even read about it and still didn't do it. Rectify your error. Do not repeat it. Lacerating self-counsel Ts him along, ears plugged with fingers against the squealing, creaking, antiquated railways of the Massachusetts Bay Transportation Authority. MBTA, vernacularly de-acronym-ed as Make Believe Train Arriving. The laws of mechanics and acoustics should embargo such screeching from such slow-moving transport, so languorous as to actualize stillness rather than motion, but no. Crawling at a speed an enwalkered octogenarian could outpace, the T grates and howls with shrill, metallic pain. The train cars: steel suppositories forced through too-narrow concrete bowels. The coder seeks the triad of parrot food, advice on feeders, and a furlough from the Mont. Synchronal catchment requires a trip downtown to confer with pleasantly useless pet store employees. Into the bird-food selections they point him, sometimes lead him by the arm. The coder feels a benignancy toward these workers. At their wages, open the store and close it. The only condonable responsibilities. Maybe watch for shoplifting. And do nothing about it. The job not worth a conk on the head nor even anxiety from a squabble. One cashier—male, glassy-eyed, twenty-five-ish, bespectacled, tattooed, goateed, emaciated, opaline, congested, sheathed in a haggard black t-shirt under a rufous polyester vest—groans with the effort of ringing up food-bags. No skin-flint, the coder. He can afford top shelf. Buys VitaNuts, JungleMix, SuperSeed, Chunk-a-Riffic victuals. And to present these upscale comestibles? The most expensive squirrel-proof feeder. Toting his loot in an oversize rucksack, the coder shifts his center of gravity, trudging unsteadily. On the T, he sits where he shouldn't: in the handicap seat. Forgives himself. Short ride. If cripples fume, they won't fume long. Montside again, he totters from the train to his car at the base of the station, which adjoins the old Suffolk Downs race-track, kaput for years. Parking on the dead-end street between? Free on weekends and post-noon on weekdays. The city concerns itself only with banning commuters from residents' spots. Good policy. All those other free hours? Can't last. Soon, the city'll wise up to the number of tickets unwritten, the amount of revenue unfleeced from citizens. Every time the coder drives to the T, he expects to see new and lambent signage. 'Party's over. Time to pay up.' Today, though, not the day. On listless thighs the coder plods to his car, tips his ruck into the trunk, sits himself behind the wheel to catch his breath and divert his heated body from excreting sweat. Food and feeder, check. Materials to suspend them, lacking. The city's stores for pet supplies sit in inconvenient relation to those for hardware. Easier to do what the coder now does: drive over the Mont to the hamlet beside it, just across the causeway. Winthrop. In esse, a peninsula. In modus operandi, an island. Whitespace for the flighters from the ever-rising Latino tide. The coder himself, superior? Never has he consciously chosen to resist the natural currents of ethnicity and race, yet he lives on the Mont, not in East Boston, not in Roxbury. The determinate? Property values. Capitalism's euphemism for racism. He did not forge the linkage and cannot alter it. Two further debilities cementing him to the Mont. Which some circles call Little Columbia. When he could live blander afield. Which some circles call Newton and Marblehead. His attitude toward the future, pasty or darker? Venga. Most paleclaves would not agree. But hardware outmaneuvers sociological debate. Between the ocean and the intervale snakes the causeway that closes during high surf and raging storms. Overhead, into and out of Logan, passenger jets graze Mont rooftops most days from five a.m. until midnight, cropdusting benzene on the natives. All residences soundproofed at state expense with quadruple-paned windows and woolpacked roofs. Autumn through May, indoors with the sashes closed, the racket recedes, speaking almost with the disjointed voice of a swelling wind. Summer? Outside? Or inside with the windows open? Shriek upon shriek of supernal machinery. The coder, like his neighbors, outdoors in summer, stops mid-sentence and restarts speech only after a jet finishes rending the welkin, yet no overflights obtruded on his parrot-concurrences. In retrospect, he credits thaumaturgy for these elsewhere-routings of planes. To what degree do placid skies embolden the bird into disclosure? The coder will need to build a spreadsheet correlating the descents of jets with future visitations. Another homebound chore he assigns himself. Can't effect it at the hardware store, which he enters with the feeder. Mechanisms of suspension? Drill? Nuts? Bolts? Armature? The coder learns. Not nuts and bolts. Screws and brackets. From such do feeders hang, in this case from the side of his house. Second floor. Between him and the clerk, productive consultations flow. Love of esoteric knowledge fertilizes cross-disciplinary nerd-yap. The coder has accessed the harmonics before. His plumber taught him how to install a toilet. His electrician, an outlet. For tutelage, watching real people surpasses video. The hardwareman instructs him on the proper manipulation of the cordless drill. He, the coder, emulates his sensei, who sends him on his way. In the car, the coder reflects on the totality of his purchases, how they make him feel. Fully armed. Never has he equipped himself so quickly and so thoroughly with sufficient steel and tools to accomplish a task, though he treats the squirrel-proof-ness of the feeder as boastful marketing. Documentaries have mentored him on the shrewdness of squirrels. Their agilities shame medal-winning gymnasts. To keep squirrels from his feeder, he must outfit himself with a weapon. In the span of a thought, a .22 abates to a BB gun to a super-squirter loaded with cayenne in solution if plain water won't rout. He will aim for those pitiless rodent eyes. Beady. Dead-black. Squirrels: rats in cute disguise. Furry tails will not stay the coder from aggression. He will mount the feeder outside the window of his second-floor office, long dumped as a generative space. Over the years, books and research journals and tchotchke, the tartar buildup of household life, conquered the territory he needed for his undertakings. The downstairs study morphed into the down-stairs office, while in the old office upstairs, an obsolete workstation shared the desk with eskers and drumlins of paper. He grades a flatness in the topography. Needs ingress to the window to mount the feeder. His excavations stir clouds of dust, and he strings on a mask until the motes calm themselves. Upstairs, not downstairs, essential, even though height can only deter squirrels, not prohibit them. Raccoons, cannier, sturdier, less prone to leap, might build a raccoon pyramid, topmost coon jouncing from the lower lip of the feeder to bring it down. The fracas, a coon-scrabbling for spoils, would wake him from a fitful sleep, so he scrapes accretions from the desk until he has cleared it for work and left the sash accessible. Plugs in the old monitor. Waits for a flash and pop, perhaps a small mushroom cloud of ozone-scented smoke. Idle for so long, the capac-itors must have decanted themselves, the circuit casings brittled. But serendipity. Cathodic humming. The thirteen-inch screen awakens after years of torpor. The coder logs in, sutures the wifi umbilicus, demits himself to this cramped outpost. Astute sacrifice for a chance at first-hand color beyond the pane. Window screen removed. Feeder hung. Again into work. Into potency and bountiful compensation.

The feeder, swaying on his periphery, violates another life lesson he has ballpeened into his children. Namely, eliminate distractions while working, for most people believe themselves superb at multi-tasking, and all people fail at it. At the tasking, not the believing. The brain evolved to fixate. Now on the predator. Now on the berries. Now on the storm. Now on the tribesman. Human attention: wired in series. For parallel, consider the nine-brained octopus and its central switching station. The coder's one-way parrot-directed tunnel kept him from checking his work-related inbox. And when he does? "Yikes." Him, aloud at his backlog. Reminds himself that he has faced worse and won and will do so again. Having thrown days at the parrot, he must now re-prioritize. Software, software. Today, Friday. Nonstop coding through the weekend should recover the slack. He notifies the house that he will soon enter a self-imposed, pro tem quarantine. No squalls of protest resound. His prowess, not just intellectual. Physical also. To sit still. To remain, not bored, not agitated, and go methodically about his errands. The overriding lesson of every artist's biography he has ever read? Stay home and do your work. This ethic, he can incarnate. From the scree, he removes a nodule. Smoothes it. Rolls it on. Selects the next to burnish. Pebble by pebble, he reposes his pile, tweezing it toward the horizontal. Bleary of eye, spastic of back, stiff of leg, weary of mind, he falters to breakfast on Monday morning. "Done it." "Done in?" His wife. "Yeah, Dad, you don't look good." His daughter. "You look like you got run over by a steamroller." His son. "All in a day's work. Or a weekend's. But look close, family, and learn. This is what happens when you get too far behind. You sprint to catch up, and you wind up bled out." "Was it worth it, the time you spent getting the feeder prepared?" His wife. "We'll have to wait and see." "No sightings while you were up there?" His daughter. "Just the usual chickadees and sparrows. A very red cardinal tricked me for a moment. I shook an admonishing finger at him." "How long are you going to leave it up?"

His son. "The feeder? As long as it takes." "Even through the winter?" His daughter. "Especially then. That's when birds need food most." "You should rig a live feed." His son. "Excellent idea." "What are you going to do if the parrot comes back?" His wife. "First, I'll take a picture." He points to his son, who fist-bumps him while chewing a mouthful of buttered wheat toast. "Then, I don't know. Throw a net over it, maybe, if I can get the window open fast enough." "You have a net?" His daughter. "No. The idea just occurred to me." "Think it through. Suppose you net it. Are you going to drag it inside while it's flapping and squawking? It'll break a wing or leg. What then?" His wife. "Same as they do with horses. Blammo." His son, who pistols his hand and fires it. "I'd turn you in for cruelty to animals." His daughter. "We're getting off track." Him. "Mom's right, Dad. If you net that thing, it's not gonna like it." His son. "Listen to your children." His wife. The coder yawns, slaps himself on both cheeks. "This is sage advice, family. Trust that I will take it under advisement. Your arguments feel persuasive." He drops the subject and trenchermans his breakfast. The house empties soon after he finishes. The feeder: monitored neither by him nor a camera as he, overcome by fatigue, sleeps until the following morning. Ts to the office. Codes for a standard shift. Researches tasteful surveillance cameras. To keep up appearances, he exchanges banalities with co-employees before decamping again for home. Mourns the discarded idea of a net. He agrees with his family that the experiment would have cratered in the resolution, but it might have thrilled in the attempt. He buffs his panes to ethereality with professional-grade, auto-detailing glass cleaners, and daytime feels charged with positivity. The parrot won't visit at night. Darkness necessitates roosting. Parrots sensible in that way. Sundown? Shutdown. Through parrotless days the coder reinstitutes customary work-life rotations. Each shift drums with software spiflications. He settles on a camera, installs it for the feeder. Has chosen a corded rather than a wifi model. Neither dead batteries nor faulty solar panels will cost him a record of a stopover. He drills a small hole in the window frame to run the cord to the camera on its fixed mount, lens square to the feeder. Remote supervision. All the while, from home or from Red Line corporatespace, he kludges up debris. His software dislodgements? Victories. Hugger-mugger to one side, order to the other. His eyes and camera treat him to woodpeckers and gray jays and sparrows and cardinals and ubiquitous pigeons and chickadees. Soon innumerable, the featheries that visit for gratis meals. His indefatigable phone aids him with identifications. Species noted, he refocuses on work, only for a flutter of color and pattern to elbow his attention again. Dark-eyed juncos and northern mocking-birds. Tufted titmice and white-breasted nuthatches. Arrive, parrot, arrive. Discard your loneliness. Companions and sustenance floweth over. His ardor radiates into a nihility. And if squirrels, nicking their ratty claws, rappel from the roof into skirmishing range, the coder flings open the sash, cleaned and greased and counterweighted for the occasion, and saturates the heisters with the gun he stores barrel-down and topped-off against the desk. The squirrels don't plummet. They register their shock. Chitter at his attack. Parkour from their banditry. Send the feeder into reckless oscillations. Squirrel bound-ings? As beyond belief as ever. From the feeder to the house to the telephone pole at the rear wall of the garbage shed. Effortless, their acrobatics. More astonishing than graceful. Wings noncompulsory for scarpering from such a height. He would not have believed it except for the evidence patent to his eyes. The airborne descent of four-legged, non-winged mammals. They land uninjured from a multi-story drop. From the ground, the squirrels look back at the feeder before scurrying off. Scouts. They'll quorum drays of the membership. Issue advisories about the two-legged crackpot who guards a roof heretofore beggared of provender. Tantalization leads to soaking and aerial self-extraction followed by hypothermia. The least they deserve. Vermin. The coder hauls down the sash. Rubs his bare arms. Returns to software. Remembers what the inrushing cold portends. The arrival of November. Knows it not by the date but by the weather. Within hours, alternating mist and rain. Only last week did the hardwoods chameleon en masse. Now this. Please no first metastasis into snow. An entreaty to climate change, which will act of its own caprice and without false advertising. Right there in the name, what it does. Sometimes colder, more times warmer, ofttimes a head-snappingly rapid transition from one to the other. But heeded, after a fashion, the coder's overture. Until near Christmas, moisture in the air snivels in droplets of varying sizes without freezing. Dreary reminder of a little-known fact. The Northeast, not the Northwest: the wettest region of the country. Precipitation across this period approximates nontropical rainforests. Those of the Olympic Peninsula, the Cascades. Also the subpolar coasts of Alaska and British Columbia. Still no parrot. The coder understands and doesn't understand. Accepts and resists. Ante-winter straitenings drove an opossum and a skunk to sortie the feeder from above. He saved the digital footage as proof. Accustomed to larder that would make Hogzilla puke, these creatures. They cannot bound like squirrels, and premonitions of Boston winters inspire quadruped melancholia. The scavengers' calculus? Climb or hang down to the feeder. Can't climb back up? Drop and die. Don't even try? Starve. Brutal, end-of-annum foistings. And the time of year, only the opposite of spring. Winter not even official yet. Pre-solstice. The frigid grip just flexing to tighten. The coder rehearses his drawn-from-life, hot-weather woolgatherings. Gouching on the beach with his family or alone. Open windows. Green branches. The lucky day when he went running and stopped for a breather beneath a tree on the seaside bottom of the Mont. As his gasping slowed, a disconcerting crackle overtook the soundscape. But no smoke to smell. No burning, circumjacent homes. The crackle, emanating from the tree itself. Biblical in import, a tree afire without combusting. Except not flames. Pinecones fracturing open.

An eruption of life. The exact right moment of the exact right day, the earliest spring day to exude real heat. Had he paused an hour earlier or later, he would have spectated nothing except the calming of his own breath in preparation for exertion again. He has tried in resultant years to pinpoint the budding of those cones. Wants his family to hear life breaking out. Has so far failed. Wants to show his family the parrot. Has so far failed. From headquarters, he monitors the feeder. Opens an extra browser window. Shrinks and foregrounds it where it won't interrupt the tasks he administrates elsewhere on his screen. Superfluous window. Colleagues who notice it, ask him about it. He happily paints the germinal evening. The heat that preceded it. His expectation of a rat. The hijinks leading to the feeder and its camera. Humanizes him to narrate his domestic maladroitness. He stretches the shrunken window for his colleagues' behoof. Better view. Most times of a feeder deserted, though occasionally flicked by chickadees' wings. His colleagues make noises of understanding, appear to approve of his hobby. The coder, a birdwatcher. Who'd a thunk it? They return to their work. He returns to his own. Deflationary, the endings of these exchanges. Animates him to speak of the parrot. Conducts him to the edge of excitement. Why? Paramount, the rarity of the emotion. Poles apart from inanition. Ataraxy of heart. Theorizes that the parrot offers pushback against skulking lassitude. Yet the parrot? His thing. Not his colleagues.' And their thing? Not his. Among the qualities his life lacks: solidarity, sodality. Perhaps what pains him so. Leads to routine. The more routine, the less pain. This relation, second only to his heartbeat among his biorhythms. Up in the morning with the kids and the wife. Assist with breakfast and the gathering of trappings for work and sundry. Wife and kids shepherded out, the coder Ts to Government Center should he decide to commute. There, a change from Blue Line to Green. Change again at Park Street from Green to Red. Hubbub with the eggheads and hipsters. Return to street level. Walk to the office. Wake the workstation.

Open the feed. Quick-scan the footage from the near-hour of travel. Register disappointment at the null result. Register also diminishing disappointment, for parrotless weeks upon months upon seasons condition him, increment by increment, away from expectation and toward desirelessness. He comes to inhabit an unremarkable stasis. His work, he effectuates as before. Of the molecule, he partakes as before. Birds visit the feeder, assorting with nature's junctures. Thaw and frost. Bloom, maturation, senescence. *The* bird? Semper absit. The anniversary of his first sighting speeds by, then autumn. The saturnine cusp of winter draws near again. Depressing. And long past time to grant the argument. The parrot: gone. Irretrievably. His wife and children have held so for many months, as, in truth, did he in his most secret heart. Hope's reservoir: drained. Claw the sand and proclaim, which a man must do who labels himself a vertebrate. The coder unrigs the feeder and camera, packs both away. Ignores the armature. To remove it would just leave screw-holes open for water to seep in and cause leprosy in the frame. He does not vacate the upstairs office, for he has grown used to the view, and the room has proven itself surprisingly incubative. His productivity through his time of residence? Upticked by high single-digit percentages. His bonuses responded in step. Mysterious battery, this overcluttered second-floor space. Left alone for so long, it must have gathered verve. The coder will siphon its voltage, then abandon it again to recharge. For a week, birds with good memories visit the space where the feeder once hung. Another month. The nadir of a Boston winter. January and February, two planished troughs of dismality. The weather, as a rule damply vile until May, can at least not curb the strengthening sun, still bright out by end-of-business hours on Valentine's Day. Luminosity to chew on and swallow as manna. Power-giving, this light. And sleep-corroding. How residents of far northern and southern climes carry on through extremes of daylight and darkness, the coder cannot fathom. Sunlight: cross-purposed. Enhances both drive and sleeplessness. On a March night, he lies in bed as his wife hibernates. Then, with a minimum of ruckus, he rolls back the covers and sits up. Rotates to rise without waking her. With his fingertips, he massages his eyelids, coercing phosphenes. He throws on his bathrobe and proceeds across the hall, toward the groaning board of his accounts. Closes the door to the office. Marinates in eigengrau. Flinches at the glare of the monitor as he wakes it. His eyes adjust. He opens his spreadsheets. Luxurious. Plenteous. He strolls a lush financial field. Skims his hand along upper ripenesses. The soft beards of anthers brush against his palms. He surveys his acreage, tracks a furrow to survey more. Annuities. Checking accounts. Savings accounts. College funds. Trading accounts. IRAs. Inspects this credit for fraud, that debit for peculation. Cannot suppress a low drumroll of disaster. Could happen. Hacked and embezzled. Nigerian princes: fictional nobles, non-fictional cutpurses. Bottomless online cesspit of scapegraces, varlets, snollygosters, hools. But nothing amiss. No tripwires in the footnotes, no claymores in the prospectuses. Every cent slips into its proper slot. Flush, every account, and never more so, yet no mollification attends on his multitudinous wealth. He gets up. Paces. Security *creates* fear? If he accepts that notion, which he rejects, he would have to countervail it, which he cannot, because he possesses abundantly fear's putative antidote: security. His heart gallops. He sits back down. His hands find his face and cover it. He remembers the yogic engrossment with breath. Return to it always. In through the nose, out through the mouth. For minutes, he repeats. His heart stabilizes. He uncovers his face. The screensaver? Retro. White dots disperse from the centerpoint of an otherwise black screen. Creates the illusion of jaunting through outer space. And save for these simulated asterisms, murk has befallen the room. His eyes, dark-adapted as in an observatory, can see without straining. In an effort to cajole sleep, he decides to read something not from a screen but from paper. Swivels for the light switch. Freezes halfway through the one-eighty.

Hanging upside down from the feeder armature? The parrot! The coder imprisons a yelp. In the adamantine beak, an inky, crustose tongue dainties a gleaned seed. Bran falls as the ebon eye pins him. Outlandish, the chiropteral suspension. Unheard of. Un*read* of. Bats hang to capacitate flight. Legs and wings—mammal legs, mammal wings—too weak to expedite ground-based takeoffs and landings, but birds evolved out of this problem tens of millions of years ago. Anatomically baseless, the parrot's inversion, and trying to make sense of it hammerlocks the coder in place. Yet he knows he must move. Believes he has reached a moment of crisis. *The* moment. Believes that how he negotiates the next seconds will determine the way he looks at himself from now until the cold earth reclaims him. He must force his body to close the distance, open the window, and *ask*. What? Something consequential. He assures himself that if his own movements don't scatter the bird, the opening of the window will. By reaching for the possibility of communion, he'll destroy it. The danger, in short, will soon pass, and at his leisure. The parrot awaits his gambit. He himself awaits it. The coder rises, dilatory, from his seat. The parrot intermits all motion. No more beak-fidgeting, no more pendulating. Capsized frozen watchfulness as if taxidermied. The coder's rise continues. He finds his feet. Urges his seat backward just far enough to create clearance for his hazardous step proximate. He must access the window. At every beat of his heart, he expects the bird to abscond. Negligent, he bumps the desk, which judders on the hardwood floor. The parrot drops from the armature. Vaporized in tandem: the coder's dread, the coder's hope. His body and mind unclench. He stands at the glass that severs him from a night bathed by streetlamps. On the upper pane, a circle of condensation now expands, now retreats as he breathes. Stilling his hands, the coder clasps the sash. Lifts. Raindrops mizzled with snowflakes gust in. He juts his torso out. Scans. The non-noteworthy house next door, the bordering vegetation, his garbage shed below: all he sees. The low thumps of a passing train, the distant bark of a dog, a far-off siren: all he hears. Re-domiciles his body. Stands for a trice in the gelidity of the still-open window. Wants his mental fixtures to desist from havoc. The parrot intercedes. Returns talons-first from the air, an advent of such bellicose aspect that the coder's instincts throw him backward onto the floor. His hands clutch at his abdomen. His innards, those talons' target? Not so. Rather the armature, where the parrot now perches right-side up. Its feet: alarming and reptilian. Its toes: snake-long and constrictive. Its talons: sickle-hooked and sturdy. In its face: an ache to slice flesh, feast on eyes, lap blood with a maggoty tongue. Coiled, erect, the parrot cocks its head to one side, then the other. The coder inches toward the window. The parrot hunches its wings, hops to the sill. Diminutive breathy streamings from the bird. The coder's own lungs and diaphragm: shoaling. And his heart? Less a biotic pump than a hank of meat vibrating from adrenaline. The coder wants to speak. Cannot. The bird must sense his anticipation, his need for utterance, any utterance. The strain of silence impels the coder to change position. At the window, he rests on his knees. Risks curling his fingers over the sill. The parrot allows him this presumption. Eye-contact between them, never wavering. Should I reach out further? The coder to himself, voicelessly, but the bird, its head, its movement, unmistakeable: *a nod.* The coder extends his left hand to stroke the patulous, versicolored feathers. And the parrot perches on his forearm. The bird shoves its head toward his. Formidably close, the stygian eye. The obsidian pupil, not a circle. Jagged along the inner ridge of the iris, a ring of flame-orange, flame-yellow. The coder feels spiked by an electrified bodkin. It prickles his optic nerve and sends a jolt to his amygdala. His palms sweat. His body rigidifies with the hours-in tautness of a corpse. Upon his horripilated skin: claws that could cause red rivers to gush. Yet only the sorriest victim, the weakest opponent, travels in mute paralysis to its final reward. Even a clam knows how to spit in protest. And so, courage. The coder must muster it. He should close his eyes. Two slashes of that beak could reap and puncture the firm grapes of his vision. But he gambles, supplicating with expressions. Explain! What next? Show! Humiliation laves the ice of his fear. The parrot lurches to its original position. Releases him from accusation. Gazes toward defenestrated reaches. Its head and nape ruffle into fullness. The tongue emerges and retreats. The beak clicks twice. Upon one leg the parrot balances. Grooms its cape feathers. Stands again on two legs. And screams. Neither panicked nor earsplitting. Whispered. Female. Strangled to the farthest reaches of audibility. Recrudescent diapason of pain inconsolable. Bloodcurdling contagion in the air above an extemporized grave. The coder will attribute future dysregulated nights to having audienced this scream, which all but compels him to outpour tears. He will not endure a second hearing, yet he continues to prop the bird even though an arm-shake would shoo it. The air it takes in, preparation for a repeat and augmented performance? The coder readies himself to implode with sorrow. He will fall prostrate before the scream or die of sadness. He awaits the ultimatum. But the parrot cedes its perch. Aviates once more. Embraces the night. Scouring for the bird, the coder beetles through the open window and almost topples to the concrete below. Adrenalized, he retracts into the room. His sweat sublimes, leaving him preserved, distraught, and slumped on the floor. What has he done, when, and to whom, of what law has he run in ignorance afoul, that justifies his victimization? If the parrot's talons on his limb constituted an arrest, he ought to recall some villainy he perpetrated. Then again, why assume justice when *injustice* rules human affairs? His run of good fortune might end here. In harassment without cause. In detainment without indictment. Do not deny the intimations. Apply science to them instead, for science predicts. Doesn't predict? Not science. Some other non-science stuffing of time. The coder must situate his experience. The parrot has returned. Did it wait for the camera's removal? Either that or Gaussian effusions acted as repellent. Long known, that some birds navigate by the Earth's magnetic field. Perhaps parrots, like cartilaginous fish, decipher voltaics for plunder and carnivory. He hasn't read of birds with ampullae of Lorenzini, and dissection should turn up electroreceptive jelly almost by default, but undocumented-ness doesn't count as disproof. Consider the protracted delay in authenticating avian reactivity to ultraviolet light. How did the coder not foresee the dispersant potential of technology? He gets up and, this time more conscientiously, leans far out the window. Cranes his neck around. Sees nothing. Withdraws. Closes the window. Returns to the bedroom. Kneels down on his wife's side of the bed. Places a hand on her. "Hon, hon. It's back." She remits garblings from the sedative of sleep. "The parrot. It's back." She claws high enough onto the shores of wakefulness to pat his cheek. "Baby, some of us have to go to the office in the morning. Some of us can't work from home." The coder, torn between excited and crestfallen, drapes his arm over his wife's hip. "I should have waited?" "Yes, but look on the bright side. Your colleagues probably thought you were crazy before. Now you've got proof you're not." "I don't. I took the camera down a while ago, remember?" The tides of sleep reclaim her. The coder rises. Backs from the bedroom. Closes the door. Stands in the hallway. Should have veiled the camera and its signals. Should have developed workarounds. Simultaneously, he believes his actions correct. Retaining the camera in the face of so much nonexistent evidence would have demonstrated his slavishness to fantasy. Worse than that. Middling fantasy. More compelling unobservables? Passenger pigeons. Tasmanian wolves. Dodo birds. Giant ground sloths. Cave bears. Smilodons. Woolly mammoths. The prodigious clade of Dinosauria. Parrots? Laughably lowly by comparison, yet the coder cannot accept the bird's secession. He must pursue. The notion of slithering back to bed appalls him. He goes downstairs. Snaffles up his phone. Won't wake. Dead battery. Forgot to plug it in. Throws the phone aside. In the kitchen, he fossicks in the junk drawer for the old point-and-shoot camera. Finds it beneath the scissors and rubber bands and plastic bags and wire ties. Flips the switch to check for life. The power bulb emits a steady green. Camera-ed, hatless, en-robed, pajama-ed, and slipper-shod, he exits the house. Slush and ice rime weathercoat his soles as he gains the sidewalk. Nothing askew in the streetlamped, halogenized darkness, just the same neighbors' houses as always, though now he scrutinizes them for nooks and alcoves incongruously sheltering a compact and flamboyant spectrum. Disappointing how many of these homes, large houses with ocean views, have incurred rotting porches, scurfy siding, rubbled stairs and sidewalks, water-damaged masonry. Once neglect gathers the momentum of blight, financial wisdom eschews repairs and dictates an up-from-the-dirt rebuild. But these Mont homes message the complements of slumlordism and appeal. The Mont, T-serviced and still cheap against other Boston precincts. No point in fixing anything when dilapidation doesn't affect demand. Renters don't do upkeep, and shouldn't, and a dearth of funds for maintenance: the bane of owner-occupiers. Visceral, the coder's sympathetic acquaintance with the exorbitant cesses and costs of homeowning. Borrow or buckle to the rapacious gentrifiers who with vulpine snouts dab airborne tracelines for whiffs of rot, then converge to mangle the source. The coder shudders, wishes his ramshackle neighbors would ask him instead of a bank for a loan. They'd find him susceptible to any reasonable request. Couldn't promise interest-free, but could promise better-than-a-commercial-bank. "If someone asked me to do it, I would." Him to his wife, months ago. "No one's going to ask." "But if they do?" "Fine by me." "No argument?" "No need. It'll never happen." "I wouldn't just start handing out checks. Someone would submit a proposal, walk me through the renovations. I'd pay the contractors, not the owners. Remember back in the day when we got heating assistance? The money went to the oil company, not to us. That's how I'd do it." "I know, but that's why I'm not worried." "You don't think people want a good deal?" "They want a good deal, but they don't want to grovel to a local rando to get one. People go to their families or banks for money, not to wealthy programmers who live down the street." He muses on his wife's rectitude as, of their own volition, his feet trek downhill. He scans rooftops and gables and the underlips of eaves and dormers as he loses altitude in the direction of the T station. Hears the clacking of wheels on tracks. The near-to-last clacking of the night. Past the witching hour, but not by much. Still early-to-bed, early-to-rise, the local Yankees. Accentuates provinciality. Twenty-four-seven service, the bedrock principle of any city with world-capital aspirations. The human project merits nothing less. Not forever will rodomontade about history and universities beguile the ambitious. Eventually, Boston will have to level up or step aside. The train wheels fade. The coder stops. His thoughts expand through the ensuing silence, fill it, and return to him. *The T! The station!* He tries to run. His slippers act in accordance with their design and name. He skids on the fog-deposited black ice of the sidewalk, then slows to the maximum speed sanctioned by his footwear. His un-cushioned soles land hard on the ground, and the last fellside of the street tilts into a steep rink. From the Mont, two exits. Rightward, to the beach. Leftward, to the T station. The coder heads left. The station, well-lit yet dingy with steel and faux marble and glass blocking and soot, presents itself as an ideal habitat steganographied by its urbanity. To survive the winter, a parrot needs warmth and shelter. T stations provide both. And food? Ecco. The donut shop beneath the elevated tracks. Crumbs and icing-ed castoffs and dumpster raids would more than suffice for fodder. Why then no neighborhood talk of the parrot? Heteroclite adaptation. Thrust into an unfamiliar environment, the parrot forsook its standard diurnalism and nyctophobia and tailored itself with darkness. Now a noctambulist, it waits for Boston to sleep, then waits for all resident scroungers to rake their territories for vittles. From its aversion to cameras and fuss, the coder surmises the bird's respect for seniority. It wishes to move about invisibly, not beef with mammals over turf. Dross galore for everyone. Irregular windrows through the streets. Equitable takings depend on the exploitation of respective competitive advantages. The parrot's? To wangle what the wingless leave behind and to access also what they can't reach. Arbitration of spoils will proceed in executive chambers. Beneath platforms. Between walls. Under trucks padlocked within fenced enclosures. And in the dark. Anywhere human eyes can't pry. Anywhere a savage beak can serve as cutlass. And unlike the kangaroo, panda, gorilla, Komodo dragon, and giant squid before their western averments, the parrot doesn't have to surmount centuries of relegation to myth. One macaw's flair for surreption shouldn't move anyone to incredulity. At the intersection, the coder jaywalks through scanty late-night traffic. Beneath the tracks, he enters the station. Stops before the fare gates to case the interior roof. One of the entrance doors behind him doesn't shut. Outdoor drafts rush through his threadbare coverings. He reties his bathrobe and buries his hands in his armpits for warmth. His eyes: probing, searching instruments. No parrot yet detected, just the large-diameter pipes that rise from the foyer to the embarkation platform. Heating-conduit fascicles transporting fluids warmer than the exterior environment. Needs to lay his hands on the metal to certify. Can't from where he stands. The pipes, on the distant side of the fare gates. His T pass, among the items he left at the house. Cannot legally access the platform, and the kiosk hosts a bowed-over transit worker who neither lifts his head from his smartphone nor glances in the coder's direction. He, the coder, could scale the gates, but not nimbly, and his inexorable rumpus would attract the worker's attention. And said worker, though to all appearances benumbed by mediocrity and the low-energy demands of a late shift near the end of a line sparsely traveled at night, wields power. One-touch contact with the authorities. The coder doesn't want to test the trigger. The worker's job: spherically dull. Soporific. The coder, similarly employed, would opt for a book over a phone for companionship, yet phones provide interlocutors. Propitiations of loneliness. And the coder knows not to mistake boredom and solitude for passivity. Spurs to action, just as easily, should he, the coder, furnish an excuse. Might wind up tackled. No better distraction than buttonholing a Bostonian erroneously believing he doesn't have to pay for a ride. Do transit workers hold legal license for seizure and arrest? The coder wants to dog the parrot, not sustain assault and injury. Clashing, his multifold appetites. Whence the temptation to birdwatch at the risk of incarceration? An absurdity even to perpend the idea. With each second, the coder calls on reserves of self-restraint. His family. His house. His career. His reputation. All potentially tarnished by a misdemeanor label of foolishness. And barred to him, the excuse of substances. Drunk? High? Neither. If he commits, he commits soberly. Then, felicitous happenstance: nicotine addiction. The transit worker stows his phone, exits his kiosk, and from one of his capacious cargo pockets extracts a fresh pack of cigarettes. He strips off the plastic wrapper. Drops it crinkling to the floor. Makes no move to retrieve his litter. Tamps a cigarette on the upside meat of his thumb. Dips his face to a lighter's flame. Steps outside and to the right, the direction of the now-closed donut shop. Breaks all sightlines. The fare gates? Too lofty for a hand-plant and side-vault, too wall-like for a slide-through or shimmy-under, so the coder clambers atop the bollardy base that registers cards and tickets. He crests the high plastic panels and tumbles down the other side, struggling to stand, tractionless in his slippers. He looks back through the foyer toward the street. The transit worker: still beyond sight, still derelict. The coder strides to the pipes. Palms them. Warmth confirmed. Above the stairs' first landing, despite mesh and fencing and dissuasive spikes on the underside of the roof, birds congregate. The city regards them as feathered, nuisance homeless, but nature resists hindrance. Adapts in most cases with a speed far outpacing bureaucracy. Birds can roost anywhere, and his bird, a wizard over famuli, can suss and circumvent with commensurate savvy. Guano on all the flights and landings. Beneath the platform's cap: tightly woven monofilament that looks throwable as a cast-net for bait. Perhaps this dauntment once impeded birds, but holes have opened in it large enough to admit individuals if not flocks, and the raddling serves as a durable foundation for nests. From one end of the platform to the other, the coder spies weedy disks above. Waiting passengers? Only four. Sight-wise oblivious to the pre-recorded announcement of the inbound train's arrival. Pairs of chickadees and trios of pigeons carry out sleepy patrols. Cheeping reaches him from an unseen source. Factitious illumination tricks chickens into laying. Tricks other birds into nighttime song. Above the netting, close to the pipes, the parrot could, must, roost. The train arrives, resorbs its fragments, departs. The coder, head tilted up, shifts continuously about the platform. The escalator delivers two pre-boarders. One walks uptrack, the other down. Befuddled, the coder wonders if the schedules have changed. These newcomers, traveling inbound, the only direction possible from this platform. But the last inbound train has just arrived and left, hasn't it? At this hour, no one but T workers should populate the station, yet on the men that flank him: normal streetwear. No clipped-on IDs. No hi-vis T-worker fabrics. Present why? He knows his own reason but doesn't feel like broadcasting it. Quashes his city-dweller instinct to ask after the trains. Undeserved, urban areas' reputation for conversational chilliness. Need directions in Boston or New York? Ask a native. Receive an oration. Locals thrill to display their command of parochial minutiae. But he, now, must focus on every joist and crossbeam. He canvasses the elevated, perch-perfect branchings of the roof. Parrotless, every nook and niche. He descends to ground level. Crosses the station beneath the tracks. Ascends to the outbound platform for a mirroring audit. Nothing and nothing again. On the far platform, a train arrives and consumes the two waiting passengers. Undercuts his confidence. He believes himself gifted with reliable instincts about time, about both its nature and passage. Now he'll have to revise his assumptions, perhaps overturn them. More uncertainties. Perfervid, his addlement. At the uptrack end of the platform, he touches the fence that blocks pedestrians from the rails. He about-faces and proceeds to the downtrack fence, touches it, walks back to the uptrack end. His movements force late-winter air through his diaphanous garments. His teeth knock together. His motivations: thrown into a war of all against all. His body shakes for indoors. His mind presses for outdoors. His guts bawl for hospitable temperatures. His heart longs for victory. This itinerant parrot must bow to proper formulations. Consider the prevalence of calories. In his short time on the platform, the coder has identified rumps of candy bars, carcasses of sandwiches, rinds of oranges, and half-eaten slices of pizza on paper plates. Smorgasbord. But a streak of irresolution bolts through him. Gently with the top of his fist, he socks himself on the forehead for his inability to remember whether macaws can feed multifariously. Monophagous in the wild, some animals turn omnivorous when deracinated and transplanted, even garbage-omnivorous, as past generations of Yellowstone bears can attest. But macaws, among the creatures that will starve if a feast doesn't include the cuisine demanded by their genetic programming? He knows the answer. Why can he not now reference it? "Indehiscent." Him, imagining edible fruits with hard loricae that don't open to release seeds. Marks the eccentricity of the word and its sudden eruction from his vocal chords. Shifts his eyes for onlookers. None. Reminds himself to tighten his impulses. The warm pipes emphasize another of his errors. He never outfitted the feeder with a heater. No wonder the parrot preferred the T station. Heater precedes feeder, or should, for organisms freeze long before they starve. The coder grows heavy with folly. His feet slow, then stop under the burden of aggregate guilt. Once home, after re-installing and refilling the feeder and subjoining it to a heater and re-mounting the camera and retrofitting it with electromagnetic shielding and recommencing around-the-clock surveillance, he will countenance the rolling eyes of his wife and children. Opprobrium: what rains upon every claimant who bucks a paradigm. And his hinky claim, now even hinkier. Not only that the unseen-by-everyone-except-him parrot has returned, but also that it perched on him and screamed whisperingly into his face. The same scream he can't stop hearing. Then, on the platform with him: the transit worker and a policewoman. Didymous public servants, side by side. How has this two-person wall erected itself? And when? And does it fear him? Or he it? Cannot discern yet which. Nor whose emotions take precedence. Nor over what. Perhaps immaterial compared to somatic considerations. The coder trembles in the cold. His skin might as well lie unprotected for predatism. Across his face: wetness where snowflakes land and liquefy. The officer, cagey, steps toward him. Right hand on the stock of her still-holstered gun, left arm extended with palm up and fingers spread. Inspiriting and ominous at once, her eloquent body. The coder flounders to process the advancing microevents. Perhaps the officer's gestures reflect a picaroon behind him. He turns and looks. Nothing but an empty platform. "You missed the last train." Police. "Station's closing. We gotta make sure no one's left before we go home." Transit. "Do you *have* a home?" Police. The question, so from-the-hinterlands, mutes the coder's response. "If you don't, I can take you to a shelter. It's not far, just down by Maverick. Not a bad place to spend the night." Police again. "Helluva lot better than outside." Transit. "Don't be ridiculous. I live right up the street." Him, evidently with unexpected cogency. Police removes her hand from her sidearm, hooks her thumbs over her belt. Transit scratches beneath the brim of his hat. "You're underdressed." Police. The coder feels accosted and disinclined to speak. These interruptions have unwoggled him from his search. No more shivers. Now a violent racking. "You got a car?" Transit. "Anything in your pockets I should know about?" Police. The coder opens his arms wide. Police pats and snoops, the camera not of interest. "How about I drive you home?" The coder's slippered soles conform to the slatted stairs of the escalator. Airiness and mechanized unforgiving-ness in the sensation. "What got you out here tonight?" Police. "I was looking." "For who? Did you find him?" Transit. "Or her?" Police. "Or it or what?" Transit. "Am I being arrested?" "Should I arrest you?" The coder doesn't elaborate. Police asks for his name. He gives it. She leads him, an alleged wight, from the station and toward the squad car idling, roof lights twirlingly ablaze, in the street beyond the foyer. Transit, near the fare gates, mutters undecryptable Transitese through his walkie as he slouches into his kiosk. Police, with her hand on the coder's back, urges him forward when they exit the station and a bear's paw of wind smites them. Sheltered beneath the tracks, fewer flakes pelt through, but the coder grunts under the sudden blow. Police ushers him into the backseat of the squad car, cupping his head against the door frame. Heat, consecrated heat. The vents exhale with powerful incinerations. Police, on the sidewalk between the car and the station entrance, pads back and forth. Speaks into her own walkie, not hand-held. Affixed to her left shoulder, the squarish mouthpiece. She reaches up to key it with her right hand. Tilts and angles her head to address it. Waits for a response. The coder in the backseat, warming. The more warm, the more grateful. Police positions herself behind the wheel. Coldness puffs from her textiles. "You said you live nearby." "Yes." "Where? Tell me." "Go straight." He droops from the pleasure of heat. "You left the car idling." "Always. Usually with the door wide open, too." "Isn't that unwise?" "If you've gotta give chase or duck behind something, the fraction of a second it saves you might save your life." "But somebody could jump in and steal it." "You ever thought about stealing a cop car? Nobody else has either. You steal a cop car, you're either too stupid to live or too high to know what you're doing. These things are conspicuous, trackable, and we can kill the engines remotely. You'd get about two blocks before you were nabbed." "Useful tech. Turn here. Left, then left again." The Mont's streets: as monkey-puzzled as Boston's inner metro zones, the baldest declaration of the district's founding in the horse-and-buggy days. To the coder's chagrin, the swirling lights batter every passing house. No siren, though, which curtails his ignominy. "Aren't the lights overkill?" "Regulation in heavy snow like this. We need to be visible to plows." The flakes, multiplying and engorging themselves, splat and stick against every surface. On the final upslope to his house, the squad car slows to a creep. The coder could have walked home in less time. Might have frozen on the way. He peers into the thickening snow, acknowledges to himself the impossibility of sighting the parrot, peers all the harder. They arrive at his house. "I left my keys behind." "Is anyone home?" "Everyone. But they're asleep." "I can't kick the door in. We'll have to wake them up." The coder dawdles where he sits. "Sir, we need to exit the vehicle and get you in the house, if this is your house. Otherwise, we'll have to take you to the station and figure things out from there." "This is my house." Police squires him to the porch. The wind. The cold. Two rude shocks. Police knocks hard and long on the front door. Rings the bell afterward. The coder crosses his arms and buries his head, huddling. Police knocks and rings again. Muffled by the accumulating snow, the idling squad car putters and chugs. Its beacon spackles his house with patriotic colors. Footfalls inside. Lights kindle on the first floor. Embarrassment and guardedness as the door opens. The crew has turned out. His wife, fazed. His son and daughter, still half zonked. They sleep so heavily that his wife must have lit their mattresses on fire to get them down here so fast. "He says he belongs to you." Police. His wife nods. Reaches out for him. Pulls him inside. "What the hell, Dad?" His daughter. "Have a good night, folks." Police. "Thank you, officer." His wife, as she closes the door. "Dad." His son. The coder feels two thin arms around his waist, a small warm body tight against his legs. His daughter touches his elbow.

On his cheek: his wife's hand. Then her arms enwrap him. "Explain yourself." "I am not well." She rests her head on his shoulder. He can hear but not see her sniffling. He understands. Tears. Which strike him as entirely justified. Another restless night follows. In the morning, after a hot shower that lifts his blood to his skin and turns him pepper-red, his mind fluctuates between emulsified and turbid as he calls his family together. He has already rung his children's schools to inform them of his offspring's tardiness or possible non-attendance for the day. Family meeting. Cannot rush it. Does not want to. He hopes for a beneficial quadralogue, for questions and answers to questions. He debriefs all concerned. His parrot-discourse? So well-established in the house that return-perch-scream convolutions in the baseline narrative don't much distract from subjects more pressing. To wit, his actions, their extremity, the unthinking manner in which he placed himself at grave bodily risk. The coder invites his family to query his mental health, as he has done and continues to do. Given the facts, can do no other. Does he feel infirm? No, but feeling well does not disprove infirmity. Think of pancreatic cancer. Afflicted in some cases for years, victims don't experience symptoms until weeks before death. Or acute leukemia. Sometimes kills within hours of inception. And no, he does not believe that whatever afflicts him, if anything afflicts him, afflicts him fatally. He details the events at the T, and hindsight besets him with regret, for his deeds can't square with sound intelligence. Gripping one hand inside the other, he chokes up at the emotional mainstay of his family, which bandies the frostbite, fractures, and electrocution that might have resulted from his bungling. Yet the crux: what he has done versus how he feels. He acted unwisely, but non-unwell people act unwisely all the time. Every day. The world over. To their profound detriment. And they bear responsibility also, provided un-wisdom explains their actions, not unwell-ness. Does un-wisdom apply to him? Can the previous night qualify as a megrim avalanche of bad decisions fallen from a healthy mind? Neither he nor his family believe so, and their non-belief reduces them all for an interval to silence. "Has anyone else seen the parrot?" His son, returning to basics. "Not to my knowledge." "Are you even sure it's real?" His daughter. "As sure as I'm sure of this table, your hand, this chair." "Sucks that it doesn't like the camera." His son. "And the feeder?" His daughter. "Visited by just about every neighborhood bird except the parrot." "Maybe it's a toy, a robot, a drone. Maybe it's a new version of one of those balloons we saw on the computer." His son, meaning the animatronic fish-shaped mylar balloons that nowadays swim through the air at parties. Mesmerizing. Young children mistake them for living, breathing creatures. "That's not what this thing is. If you saw it, you'd agree." "But no one has seen it." His wife. "Except me." "Except you." His wife again. Heart constricted, he scans the somber, doleful faces of his family. "Hallucination." His daughter. "I don't believe it is." "But you can't prove it isn't." His daughter again. "It's hard to prove a negative." "Then prove a positive." His wife. "I tried, and not only with the feeder and camera. With the socials, too. I put the word out, but I couldn't even get a bot or troll to confirm." "At this point, you don't have a better explanation than a hallucination, so what might have caused it?" His daughter. "Any number of things. Fatigue. Confusion. Even expectation." "You have trouble sleeping, Dad." His son. "And you really want to see it." His daughter. "But this time I had insomnia from sunlight. I wasn't fatigued. I was wired. And I'd given up on seeing it. That's why I took down the camera and feeder. All I can say is, I've got no reason to think it's not real." "What about drugs?" His daughter. His wife shoots him a glance. The silent telegraphy of a long marriage instructs him not to answer, not right away. Maybe the girl will reveal on her own what she knows of this subject. His daughter registers her parents' watchful anticipation. "Are we supposed to pretend pot isn't legal in this state? It's not like we'll be shocked if you eat edibles or smoke every once in a while. Last time

I checked, you're over twenty-one. Maybe you caught a bad strain. Joints, gummies, or vapes? Somebody could have laced them with PCP or psilocybin or something. That happened to a friend of mine at school. Maybe you got stung the same way, Dad." "No. I hadn't smoked anything. I wasn't high." "Flashbacks?" His son, to three looks of surprise. "What? Even in my grade, they drum this stuff into us. So boring." "Flashbacks don't apply." The quiet that follows this response: some form of adjournment, though no one retires from the table. The ensemble sits awash in unresolvedness. Anxiety. Aphasia. Real life. "This doesn't have to be the end of the discussion. In fact, it shouldn't be, but it seems like for now, it is. Get your stuff together, and I'll take you to school." His wife, savior of the situation. The off-spring groan as they give their father a hug and leave the room. His wife clasps his hand in commiseration. "I left out some possibilities." Him. "Schizophrenia. Tumor. Generalized psychotic break." "We can probably rule out schizo. That would have kicked in fifteen or twenty years ago." "The leftovers are not inspiring." "No, they're not." "You're sure about flashbacks?" His wife, after looking at the ceiling, where both children remain on the recto, readying themselves for school. "Positive. The body burns up the molecule almost on contact. Even if we were talking about LSD, which is way more long-lasting, flashbacks are essentially an urban legend." "What do we do now?" The kids recur, backpacked and shod. "Get them to school. I'll start planning." His wife and children exit, and he begins wading through Boston's mire of physicians. Calls and calls. All these doctors and no appointments? His nation: sicker than he imagined and in more ways. Nexus of maladies, this country. For the coder himself, fat chance of a timely diagnosis. His history of rugged health inflames the maddening protractions of answer-seeking. "Nothing sooner? That can't be right." Him, upon the proposal of yet another seasons-away appointment. "A lot of people need care, sir." The scheduler. "How many? Boston isn't that big. Philly could put us in its pocket, to say nothing of New York." "I can only present you with our options, sir." "I should stab myself in the skull and traipse into an emergency room. I'd get immediate care then, wouldn't I?" "You would, but I wouldn't advise that course of action." On hold, he envisions the scenario, hilt left to protrude, a jump-the-line pass to the top of the triage chart. Not even his private funds can speed his campaign. The more prestigious the doctor and institution, the more booked-up. Every gatekeeper adjusts not by one iota the appointment machinery. In the city, only so much diagnostic equipment. Only so many days on which it toils. Only so many technicians to operate it. Only so many doctors to evaluate output. Only so many insurance companies to screw the insured. He accepts the soonest-available slot, puts himself on the waiting list in the event of a cancellation, then hangs up and ingeminates the procedure with a different office. To exorcise his family's vexation, he will welcome with a generous heart every curative usurpation. He and his wife agree not to worry unless someone with a medical license ratifies pathology. "Like repeated encounters with a parrot?" Him. "Stop it." Her. "Do *you* think I'm psychotic?" "I told you, I don't know what to think." "What's your instinct?" "You're not psychotic." "I'm going to hold you to that." The months accrue as his tests, scheduled in the benthics of upcoming time, rove for abyssal prey before turning skyward. The coder handholds to the fin of each whale as it achieves the surface and blowholes data. When no insights rain down, he lets go and waits for the next slow-rolling breach. Treads water. Works. Codes. Searches. First boolean result for 'parrot scream' yields a paragraph of reasons for various parrot vocalizations. Abounding results to 'why does my parrot scream,' but all on normal parrot screams, which attain decibel levels and vibrations sufficient to pulverize brick. Appending the oxymoronic 'whispered scream' to 'parrot' yields parrots that whisper and parrots that scream and no parrots that marry the two actions. These disobliging searches: tip-offs of tech's incapacity to clarify anomalies marginalized by algorithms. Good record-keeping helps him avoid repetition. Sampling the guazzabuglio: 'parrot scream whisper' yields help with quieting a parrot, 'parrot scream whisperer' yields an eponymous swindler, 'parrot pain' yields results similar to ones on stopping a parrot from screaming, and 'parrot murder' yields a string of offbeat stories. Parrots as witnesses, and not just to life. To crimes. In Detroit, for example. Prosecution? Wife murdered husband. Defense? No, she didn't. Their pet parrot, taken to repeating "Don't shoot" in the voice of the victim. The coder declines to parse the guilty verdict, for he must cope with his own predicament. *The parrot's scream, unmistakably female, narrowing sources by fifty percent, but an otiose narrowing because infinity divided by two yields infinity. Any crime, any drama, joyous as well as ruinous, might elicit a scream. From a scofflaw or victim? Participant or bystander? And from an event real or virtual? Can't overlook pure invention either. The parrot amusing itself by frightening him. Alas, resignation. The scream's provenance, undiscoverable. An impracticable task, to determine the background and present circumstances of a random, perchance figmentary, parrot. Imponderables to the side, then. To the fore, concreticities. Blood work. X-rays. MRIs. CT and PET and bone scans. Undiagnosed drug reactions could explain his deviation, but no drugs pollute him. What of previous ingurgitations? Embedded with old pills, a bezoar might squirt adventitious abnormalities into his senses. He saw this contingency once on a TV show, mentions it to his internist, who, to rule it out, adds a colonoscopy to his raft of tests. More than a year elapses before the final docking of the coder's voyage through specialized western medicine. The cumulative avouchment: normal. All the drainings of blood. All the proddings and probings. All the radiative invasions of his flesh. None dragoon into salience a single lesion, neoplasm, scar, inflammation, glandular dysfunction, neuromuscular deterioration, organ peculiarity, or tissue deformity. Stricken with the pre-existing condition of mortality, but otherwise not a gene misfiring. Utmost confidence in the decree, moreover, because to minimize false-positives and boost the viability of his cancellation-standby status, he enforced on himself through the testing period the asceticism of clean living. No drinks, no drugs. Fiber and vegetables and exercise. He filtered himself back to post-natal immaculation. Saturated fats, replaced with unsaturated. Simple starches, swapped for complex. The demon caffeine, out. The devil salt, its dogsbody dairy, rusticated. The humble, energy-giving lentil achieved dominion over his carbohydrates, supplanting fruit, the intake of which good nutrition does not require, given correct vegetable consumption. The slogan of his one-man revolutionary movement? Sugar equals poison. Fructose, a variant. Exiled. His changed habits, with which he persists post his corporeal testing stage, evoke plaudits at the office, where he appears with increased regularity to shore up the notion of all-around health and wellness. Ministers furthermore to his mind. Shrives at first with a psychiatrist *and* a psychologist. At his initial sessions: fast briefings on the symptom that forced him to their doors. Enlightenment-oriented Eightfold Paths, noble or otherwise, do not wend forward. He explains about the parrot and its possible hallucinatory essentiality, his skeptical openness to that idea. "Though you're the expert." Him, terminating his synopses. Gets evaluated against a checklist for depression, anxiety, insomnia, malapert episodes, compulsions to self-harm including but not limited to suicidal ideation, and sexual deviance, which the lexicon now connects to statistics rather than morality. "Deviant means only a trait or behavior or opinion that the majority does not share. Civil rights for black people were once considered a deviant idea." The psychologist. "They still are." Him. "Vaccination used to be controversial-slash-deviant." The psychiatrist. "It still is." Of the tags both psychs try to press on him, the highest-static one that clings best? Recurrent thoughts. "And if the parrot *isn't* a thought?" Him. "For the sake of diagnosis, let's assume it is, but either way, it doesn't matter much." The psychologist. "How's that?"

"What matters, what's significant, is how it affects your life, whether it disrupts it in a negative way. Real things can do that. Imagined things can, too. What's important is the disruption. If we can get *that* under control, its source might become more manageable. We might even get it minimized to where you can ignore it altogether." This reconceptualization whipsaws him. Scotches also the psychologist's colleague, the one with the prescription pad. Opposition to him: the coder's inclination after a pair of visits, though less the fault of the practitioner than of his discipline. The psychiatrist's degree connotes a fearsome quantity of assimilated lab-coat know-how. Mobilizes the coder's fraternal vestiges. Undergrad for him and the psychiatrist: long indenturements to rigor. Equations. Latin. And the increase in difficulty with each passing year? Not arithmetic. Logarithmic. The language arts, the humanities, can't measure up. Tolstoy reads as easily as Salinger. Just takes longer. Maybe takes more discipline. But in terms of knowledge, any precocious eighth-grader can accomplish the task. The question that separates undergrad fun from undergrad gravitas: must you calculate? Pre-med answers with an unambiguous yes. Yet conversance with substances and a license to prescribe them cannot automatically stand in for an ability to diagnose and treat an ailment efficaciously. With the psychiatrist, the coder expects a discussion of his supposititious ailment, then a discussion about whether it requires treatment, and only then a discussion about how to treat or cure it, but the psychiatrist leaps over exhaustivity, sticks a landing on medication. "Talk-therapy isn't really what psychiatrists do anymore. We go right for prescriptions and properly balanced dosages." Two strokes for honesty. Disposes of pettifogging and faff. Upon the close of the consultation, the psychiatrist gifts him a list of medications to read up on for pharmacons and side effects. Research! The coder scholarizes himself to the fine print ignored by pillheads. Maftir to the haftarah, his relation to the concoction-documents he studies before entertaining the ingestion of even a single caplet. Un-surprising side effects. Headaches. Dry mouth. Dizziness. Nausea.

Weight gain. Weight loss. Fainting. Sweating. Internally generated electroid shocks to the head and brain, colloquially termed the zaps. Skin rashes. Irritability. Fernweh. Acedia. Itching. Bloodshot eyes. Constipation. Diarrhea. Hot flashes. Cold flashes. Burnings and tinglings throughout the body. Paranoia. Stomachache. Flaccidity. And ejaculation long after the termination of coitus, clinically known as retarded orgasm. Endurable, all of these manifestations, save one. Hallucinations. On every pastille's rap sheet, the very phenomenon he hopes to vitiate. Takes the coder unawares, to look askance at erudition appurtenant to chemical poultices, but to the psychologist goes the laurel. The coder proceeds to investigate, evaluating mentally the strictures of her discipline. To his uberquestion, she can answer yes. She must calculate. She has published in academic journals enterable only through competence in statistical methods. The internet presents subscriber links to her analyses. He tables his concerns about turning himself, a human being, into a data point, and continues along the psychological prong of his journey. "How do I feel? Is that really quantifiable?" Him, after removing his coat and sitting down to continue his therapy. The psychologist crooks her head. Not a smile, rather a shimmer in her eyes. Knowingness? "Not the first time someone asked you that question, is it?" Him. "Would you like it to be?" "In a way. I was just thinking that every time I open my mouth in here, I show myself as un-unique." "Would that be so bad?" "Is this how it's going to go, every question answered with another question?" "No. And if therapy is about anything, it's about individuality." "I'm not sure I buy that. I'm not sure you should either." "Why not?" "Because the more similar people are, the more psychology can be a science. Physics and chemistry would never get anywhere if we couldn't predict what atoms were going to do." "You want me to predict your behavior?" "Maybe not predict. Maybe tell me what I might expect." "The only person who can do that is you." "Apparently I can't. That's why I'm here." "Do you feel that you can't control your actions?" "Not exactly, but I've told you about my T-station lapse." "On that night, did you feel compelled or under control?" "If what you're asking is whether I could have stopped myself, then, yes, I could have. I should have, but I didn't." "All right, then let's call what you did or didn't do poor decision-making and proceed under the assumption that you can control your actions." "What about my thoughts?" "There are techniques to regulate them, if you think they're out of control. Do you?" "Not aside from what I've already told you. What techniques, though?" "Meditation, for one. Prayer also works for some people." "Isn't prayer a form of meditation?" "You could think of it like that. Meditation is perhaps more inward-directed than prayer, but the benefit mostly comes from the ritual aspect." "Like the rosary." "Perfect example, though rituals, too, can get out of control. Are you Catholic?" "I was raised by agnostics. Then, once puberty kicked in, I became an atheist." "Very common in the sciences." "I used to spout Diderot. 'Man will never be free until the last king is strangled with the entrails of the last priest.' My militance faded as I got older. I don't get in people's faces anymore unless they get in mine, but the belief, or non-belief, hasn't changed. I like to think I was ahead of the curve. I went godless as a tween. The sciences just gave me supporting arguments." "What about what the sciences can't explain?" "We just say we don't know. Why are people so reluctant to say that?" "You think they are?" "You think they're *not*? Seems to me, whenever people can't explain something, they prattle on about Jesus or Allah or some other invisible entity in the sky." "You have contempt for this." "Shouldn't I?" "I can't answer that. Only you can articulate your beliefs." "Okay, yes. Contempt." "Why?" "Because it's no different than believing in Santa Claus. Fine if you're six years old, infantile and shameful if you're grown." "I see." "You don't agree." "It doesn't matter whether I agree. I don't judge. Some psychologists do, but I don't. I'm just trying to get a better sense of who you are. Guidance comes later, maybe." She probes the parrot as a hallucination, acknowledges his belief in its reality. "Problem is, the only way for me to know whether I'm correct is to verify it, but if I'm wrong, I'm trying to verify something that's not there. You think I've got a case of the crazies?" She chuckles. "That would not be a valid diagnosis." "Have you heard of anything like this before?" "Possible hallucinations? Very common. Parrots particularly? No, but that doesn't matter." "Your touchstone phrase." "If I believe something to be beside the point, I say so." "How can the parrot be beside the point?" "Because *you're* the patient. Try not to get hung up on the parrot. We need to center on you. Suppose for the sake of argument that you thought dogs were talking to you." "Son of Sam." "A famous, tragic case, yes." "Simpler than what I'm facing." "How so?" "Dogs don't talk. Guy says dogs are talking to him, you lock him up or medicate him. Or both. Open and shut. With me, there's a debate." "Remember what we talked about. Your actions are more important than what's inspiring them. You've told me, and I've got no reason to disbelieve you, that you're clear of all the factors we'd have to prioritize otherwise. Trauma, family history of mental illness, biological causes, drug use—" "Let me stop you right there." He instructs her on the molecule, on its properties and effects and non-effects. Also on his abstinence since his T-station incident. "The renunciation continues through this moment, I might add." "Sounds like wild stuff." "Beyond the beyonds." "I've never heard of it, but it shouldn't be relevant if you haven't done it in so long and there are no flashback issues." "We've returned to where we started." "No, we've gotten more truth from you, and more truth is always good, but I'm not sure this latest truth changes anything." She considers him through long seconds, no trace of anxiety. He admires this skill. He himself can remain quiet and still, but not like she can, not with her total tranquility. Minus the talent, she would fail in her profession. "Maybe I can come at this in another way. Forget about the parrot for a moment. Go with dogs and cats instead. Do you live in the suburbs?" The psychologist. "The Mont is on the T about fifteen minutes from downtown. I wouldn't call it the suburbs." "What I'm interested in is whether you're around other houses." "Practically on top of them. Thickly settled, in New England patois." "There are yards, sidewalks, fences?" "Naturally." "Children? Pets?" "You're on a roll." "Now think of those pets. Think of dogs and cats. Imagine how often you see them. Maybe not every day, but you're outside, and there goes a cat. You don't know who owns it, if anyone, but it has definitely been around before. There goes a man walking his dog. The same man, the same dog you've seen many times. And then?" "Then, what?" "That's what I'm asking. You see the man. You see the dog. And then?" "Then, nothing. I go on with my life." "And the man and the dog?" "They go on with theirs." "You don't know that. You don't know what happens to them. Maybe only seconds after you look away, something extraordinary happens to them that has never happened before and will never happen again. Why do you assume nothing happens?" "Because there's no reason for me not to. I see them, and I ignore them." The psychologist's face: not smug, but pleased. The coder needs a moment for percipience to arrive, but when it does, his incurvate spine remodels itself as a steel rod. "I ignore them, but I don't ignore the parrot. Why?" "I can't answer that, but from what you've told me, this parrot is as irrelevant to your daily responsibilities as a neighborhood dog or cat. You should be able to let it go about its business as you go about yours." "My fixation is the issue, not the reality or non-reality of that on which I'm fixated." "I couldn't have said it better myself." "Huh." Into the soft seat he now reclines. "How do you feel?" "I should feel better, but I don't." "There's no wrong way to feel." "That's not true. Drug addicts feel like they should do drugs. Alcoholics feel like they should drink. Molesters feel like they should molest. Serial killers feel like they should kill. All wrong feelings, every one." "Addiction and psychopathy are exceptional cases that prove the rule. In most instances, it's not helpful to think of feelings as right or wrong. Can you tell me why you think you should feel better?" "Because I just learned something." "Specify, if you can." "That I did this all to myself." "Why should that make you feel better?" "Because it's the truth." "And the truth is uplifting?" "The truth shall set me free. Isn't that the line?" "Yes, but freedom, truth, uplift—it can be difficult to leave things behind in order to secure them. Do you feel like you've left anything behind?" "Lies I've been telling myself." "Lies can be comforting. They can distract us from painful truths." "What truths am I distracting myself from, if I'm distracting myself?" "That's something we can investigate." "And what about lies that service the truth?" "Again, that's something we can talk about at our next session." "Done already?" "I'm afraid so." "But I just got going." "Don't worry. This gives you something to think about until next time." Two weeks distant. He scheduled bi-weekly appointments because weekly felt egocentric. Triweekly, like lollygagging. Regret for his choice now pinches him. Normal, his impatience, she reassures him on his way out. Lauds his garrulous-ness as a solid foundation. "What should I do for our next session?" "Think about the work we did today." "No, no. What should I *do*? Give me something to really occupy myself with." "What about your family, your job?" "Minor obstacles." "If you've got extra time, you could always start journaling. It's active, and it helps people organize their thoughts." "Like a diary?" "Call it what you want. It doesn't have to be any precise form, just some kind of record." "Handwritten or on the computer?" "Up to you, but research suggests that handwritten is more therapeutically effective." "Why?" "The science isn't definitive, but the pace of handwriting seems to be the crucial factor. People have to schedule time to write by hand. It forces them to slow down, and there's a calming aspect to that, also less chance of distraction. You can't click away from a piece of paper." "I hand-write so seldom, I barely remember how. Then, when I do it, I can't read what I write." "Typing is fine. Handwriting's advantage is very modest. Make a daily schedule and obey it. Give yourself a minimum word-count and meet it if you can." "What if I go over?" "That would be great, but here's a trick. If you know you're going to go over, stop, then pick up the next day where you left off. That way you'll never be stuck. And if you keep exceeding your minimum, increase it and go on from there." "But where should I begin?" "Wherever you like. Lots of people start with their dreams." "Very Freudian." "Yes, but also very practical, since most days begin with an interrupted dream." "But what if I don't dream?" "Everybody dreams sometimes. Keep a pen and paper by your bed. Wake up. Make notes. Write or type them out later. But you really must be going now. My other patients are waiting." He exits the office, buoyed by her perorations. "How'd it go?" His wife, after he arrives home. "Startling." "Bad, good?" "Not bad. TBD on good. Two weeks is a long wait. I wish I could go back sooner." "She must have ginned up a real miracle today." "Better." "What's better than a miracle?" "A project." In the morning, he quits the bed. Yawns if he slept. Wipes his face with his hands. Secretes waste in the bathroom. Refuels in the kitchen. Before doing anything else, and whether headed to work or staying home, he sits at the computer and enacts the suggested intervention. The web tempts him. Just a quick peek. Get your fix. Clear your head. Siren song. He can sing it. Can fall to it if he weakens. He, a techromancer: its lyricist. Screws on the cuirass of his pre-internet graduation into adulthood. Believes himself still fully human in that he can make and hold eye contact, carry on a conversation, read books for hours on end and remember their content. What he typed on the morning he opened his simplest text editor? 'When he dreams, he dreams of violence.' Unintended, his obscuration behind third-person. Did not overrule himself. As the subconscious dictates, follow. Which he does in the days that amass. "The violence you speak of, maybe you wish it were in someone else's dreams, not yours." The psychologist. "No argument there." His wife would spring to substantiate. Present, she'd flaunt her bruises. Between visits, the coder's journal grows. He fills a page before moving on to other tasks. Insignificant, the extent to which his private activities impinge on his corporate duties. His productivity never decreases. His project expands apace. And for weeks, then months, reality jibes with how he describes reality to himself. Appointments with the psychologist: completed. Shows her his capabilities. She intersperses her compliments with expressions of surprise that he took so readily to her suggestion, considering his background and history, both empty of similar endeavors. He reiterates his preference for tasks. "Doing something, even if it's just trial and error, counts as advancement because it beats doing nothing." Him, during a session. "And your terrors, have you noticed any difference in them?" "They're less frequent, but they wax and wane. Always have." "How long have you had them?" "A long time." He back-calculates to pin down an origin. Not courtship with his wife, nor college, elementary, and middle school. Neither the paturition of his children. Maybe some occurrences during high school, but his memories of those days feel so nebulous that he discounts them. "Did your kids sleep through the night as babies?" "No, and they hated napping, too. It was like they equated sleep with death. They were sleep-assassins much longer than they should have been." "When did they give it up?" "School. Once they got into the routine, they straightened out." "Your terrors must have begun sometime after that." He chuffs at this assessment. The retro path to clarity: so straight and of such gentle grade that he wonders why he never walked it before. He pauses to remove a volar pebble. "You said terrors, not night terrors." "Night terrors occur when you're asleep, but the parrot comes when you're awake." "You think they're related?" "It's hard to imagine they're not. They're both corrosive forces. But perhaps I shouldn't have lumped them together. I was trying to cover days, nights, asleep, awake, everything. I can come up with another term if terrors doesn't sit well with you." "Maybe hagridden?"

"If you like." "Not necessary. The word just came to me. Terrors is fine, except now I have to ask myself whether I'm terrified." "During the parrot's scream, you said you were." "Yes, but the other times, I wasn't. I was excited, curious, looking forward to more contact. All positive emotions. Is that relevant?" "Why wouldn't it be?" "Because how we feel isn't always aligned with what's happening to us. Now I sound like you. Can someone be terrified without feeling terrified? Would that be like having cancer but not feeling sick?" They plumb terror as an unfelt reality. Inward, unfailingly inward. At the milestone of two years beyond first-sight, the coder spends a session in near-silent contemplation. What he contemplates? His inability to expunge the parrot from his waking attention. He cannot integrate the psychologist's dog-and-cat comparison. The gone-ness of the parrot from his life: total and decisive. Why does he grant this animal, so unseen for so long, continued residence in his mind? He composes a mantra to dispossess the bird, flood the space it occupied, and render harmless by dilution any lingering impurities. *Gone and not returning. Gone and not returning. Gone and not returning.* His shtum, chanting portrayal of a desacralized Athos monk. The inherent contradiction of the technique, forgetting while reminding, resolves itself as the mantra drones into a narcotizing brain fug. In this way, he succeeds at forgetting, succeeds in believing the parrot will not reappear. And then it does. And when it does, the coder cannot believe it. He gets off the T after yet another session of headshrinking. Exits the fare gates and the foyer. Feels parched. Ducks left beneath the elevated tracks where a roast-beef-and-soda stand has occupied a double-wide trailer for decades. As with free street parking, so with this stand. Real estate too valuable for the status quo to last much longer. Ever-gormandizing investors will soon displace the trailer, but for now the coder buys a cola. His ice-filled cup sweats into his hand. Carbonation dapples his tongue as he nurses the straw. Swallowing, he shifts his feet desultorily. Glances across the dead-end street to the decrepit, rust-red wooden fence around the shuttered Downs. And there the parrot sits. Atop the fence. The Mont station, in keeping with his hunch, its base of operations. The slatternly Downs, good foraging grounds just adjacent. The sighting, well-lit instead of tenebrous, yet no one else nearby to corroborate. An inflection point, this moment. He can acknowledge as innocuous what he sees, turn from it, and continue with his dealings, or he can jerk the wheel of his life and steer straight for what he ought to avoid. He decides. He drops his soda and bag and makes for the fence. Lucky engineering, the dead-end-ness of the street he sprints across, for to step so heedlessly into a Boston roadway risks summary execution by an anarchic driver. His body moves in response to an urge to seize prey. Could snuff this flare. Instead, he pumps the bellows. Lusts to clamp the parrot and validate that they share the same reality, and that he, not it, rules that reality. But the parrot takes to the air, flying down, not up, flapping and dropping behind the fence into which the coder slams for want of braking distance. The splintering, flaking, red-washed slats, so close to his face upon impact that for a millisecond he smells dry-rot. Would have tasted it, too, had he crashed with tongue lolling. For all its desuetude, the fence has not relinquished its opacity. The coder fails to laser a peephole in the wood. Hands flat against the planks, he squints through this crack, around that knot. Moss and lichen stopper every crevice to occlusion. Backs away, frantic. Chainlink in a curving rampart overhangs the ridgeline of the wooden slatting. Bastion against agile looky-loos and long-extinct fans circling for ticketless entry. In their place, thieves? Stealing what? Manure residue from the quit paddocks and stalls? The coder microbursts with fury as every passing second swats him. He has already blown his therapeutic guidance. Wants at least a trophy to wave for his transgression, but above all wants to see. He cannot see. He craves the height of Marfan syndrome. Looks left and right along the grassy strip on which he stands. Road tailings. Trash in the form of food wrappers and styrofoam cups. Nip bottles wearing the earring-sized necklaces left over from their torn-off thimble caps. Not a bucket to stand on nor a log nor a defunct shopping cart. All this metropolitan detritus and nothing sturdy. Just filth on a heightless mission. Backpedals onto the street. Clears the parked cars. Jumps to inadequate apogee on the bitumen. Scans to the dead end, up the opposite sidewalk, even to the other side of the intersection. In every direction, salt flats of unassistance. His heartbeat. His shallow breaths. The seconds ticking, ticking. He squares himself to the fence. Eyes the overhang. Triangulates the ideal group of links he might reach with a vertical leap. He makes his best estimate and launches himself skyward. His fingers bayonet the mesh and suspend him. Feet dangling inches from the ground. If he can lift his crown high enough, he might see the parrot. Don't jinx with overconfidence. Pull yourself up. Have to. Use your back and abs, not just your arms. Think strong thoughts. Panting, he lets go. While hanging, he could barely kink his elbows. Shouldn't even have tried. Should've remembered his two-pull-up personal record from adolescence. Shouldn't have burned more time. Should've factored in the years of body-mass increase and arm-strength decrease and realized impending futility. The fence circles the Downs and opens only at the gates which themselves lie around a curve and at the end of a straightaway. He has never delimited the sweep before, but far on foot and with chains and padlocks assuredly adorning the gates. The draggletailed site awaits clearance for demolition. Developers will swarm in afterward and erect high-rise luxury apartments on the ruins. Until then, the coder might see through or around or past the padlocked gates. Beside him, he feels the presence of the psychologist, not with her arms crossed, not short of patience and tapping her foot, but simply watching, waiting, curious to see what he will do. Apparent to both of them, the choice he faces, the same choice he faced moments before: ignore or indulge. Apparent also, the choice he *should* make. His pulse thunders. Concussive booms thump him to the deafening ululations of fleeing time. Again, he chooses. He runs. His hardest sprint. Boyhood, the last time he ran so, and not often enough to bank the muscle memory he needs now, decades later, to vehiculate his body into such taxing motion. In his khakis and chukkas and untucked blue gingham trim-fit button-down shirt, he jinks pedestrians absent only moments earlier when he needed them for backup witnesses. He eats sidewalk en route to the first swooping lefthand turn. Too far away, this turn, and only a small part of the total distance he must cover. His body cannot handle the strain. This run demands Olympic athleticism, not the aptitudes of someone who, as a teenager and alone on a track, once tried to sprint a single four-hundred-meter lap. Wanted only to see if he could do it. He could not. He approached the third turn in a wheezing jog, crossed the finish line by pitching himself over it, then convulsed on the deserted, rubberized asphalt. His body castigated him. Pain and nausea, the prima donna and primo uomo roles of physiology. For a half hour, he felt sure someone would have to wrap him in cerecloth and warble over his clay. And now? Much farther to run. And he? Much older than the boy who failed the lesser test. Not going to end well: the coder's judgment of his own actions, even as he cleaves to them. By the first turn, he has slowed. Still feels vibrant, though, as he banks to the left, rolls smoothly, arrows forward again. Inspires vim, to move, to dash. Lashed by knouts of hope, he wrings his glands for adrenaline to compensate for his muscular deficiencies. He nears the long straightaway to the rachitic grandstand. Then it arrives: the flagging he anticipated. His legs burn and deliquesce. His lungs pump fluorosulphuric acid into his charred esophagus. He should stop running. He does not. Moils harder. He can see the grandstand, and the sight hardens his conviction that he will not reach it, not with any locomotion faster than a hitching limp, yet he pushes, pushes. His reserves dwindle and disappear and trigger drawdowns from emergency supplies. His speed has dissipated already from a sprint to a run to a trot to a yawing lurch ventilated by tearing breaths. The grandstand, marooned on an immane and vacant parking lot, bodes rest. He will have to pause before the gates. Haltingly, he moves forward. Suppresses the urge to stop, bend at the waist, vomit on his feet. From within a nimbus of pain, he tells himself that his progressions still qualify as running, not walking. Running hurts. Walking doesn't. QED. He refuses to end his ordeal. Knows he should, for it destroyed upon onset any real possibility of reaching the goal. Sealed beyond repeal, his too-late arrival at the gates. The parrot: without a doubt lost to the numberless exclaves of the air. Into the coder, every breath and step sears the certainty of failure. Continues because he started. He has raced down and captured tech all others considered illusory. This bird, arguably analogous, arguably worthy of pell-mell pursuit, but only arguable with *bad* arguments, those he and the psychologist out-reasoned. Hadn't he moved past the mindset now pillaging him? All the coaching and nudging into healthier frames of non-fixation, non-perseveration: shot down. Spectacularly so. His plodding, yomping feet. His wracked body. The coder construes his present state of operations as ill-considered and destructive. He should flip the kill switch and stop. He should sit down. He should draw up his knees or extend his legs flat. He ought to let the pressurized balloon of his skin burst, soak him all over and fetidly with sweat, bathe and cool his fissuring heart. Voluntary, all the muscles pertinent to the situation. Stop activating them. Full stop. *STOP.* But, headlonging, he ignores the chyron. Self-harm, the condition he has chosen. *The condition he continues consciously to choose.* He follows the straightaway and the fence, reaches the mid-steppe desolations of the parking lot. His feet lift from pavement and fall again to gravel and road salt and plastic bottles and kibbled glass and two old tires that he circumvents with a swerve instead of the bound he might have improvised from more advantageous physical conditioning. Far behind him now, cars idle in a line, waiting for the intersection signal to change. Ahead and in his path, half a traffic cone. Must have survived several years of freeze and thaw only to grow brittle and shear in the wind. The coder adjusts his line. Stumbles. Flails his arms to regain his keel. His gyroscopes hold him to the fence as it describes the waistline contour of the Downs. The base of the grandstand heaves into view as his corpus flirts with a full-margin rupture. His heat-stressed eyesight judders with the rigid shocks of his footfalls. His consciousness verges on exodus. To his faulty vision, add swirling, flashing, silver-white stars that crowd resolved images from his retinas. Hold. On his left, something crimson flickers above the rampart. The coder skids to a stop. Goes to the fence. Tries again to jump and pull himself up. Can't even jump. He folds in half, hands on knees, attempts to catch his breath, which won't slow for him to grab. Rather, it speeds up, as does his pulse, racing now despite his lack of motion. Panic, both description and command. His chest and midsection pummel him. In the Kalahari, the San run kudu to death as he has footwise hunted himself. His heart rate bounces upward in staged, rocketing thrusts. He retches, ejecting no food. Juices trickle into his mouth. He spits. Yellow bile. Some green. No gleeting of black nor red. His tract, not bleeding yet. He crumples, knocks his head hard against the ground. Enough force for a rebound but not unconsciousness. His heart rate apexes. On his back, the spall of the pavement gnaws at him. He feels the onrush of death and refuses to close his eyes. His own idiocy has dispatched him. He rolls to the side. Another retch and cough. The morphon of his body constricts with myogenic spasms and filtrates only air. On his back again, he stares, alight with pain, into an ultramarine sky that no clouds fleece. Then, a garnet claw mark stains the vault, a rutilant slash that extends and drips before recoiling toward the primary, levitating blot. The coder's squalling body *experiences* a sound. The parrot's voice. Another scream, but not sotto voce. This scream could drown biology's summative cacophony. To the coder's pain, add now a sucking dread. That he has tracked the parrot and found it: something to regret, and maybe false. He himself, perhaps the lured and latibulated. The parrot banks out of straightline flight and circles not in the flapless way of soaring albatrosses upon seawinds, nor of condors snatching cliffside gusts, but rather with the wingbeats of a raptor aligning for a stoop. More vocalizations reach the ground. The screeches of an owl. The cries of an eagle. The parrot completes a last tight turn and barrel-rolls into the vertical. Through the dive, which relativistically foreshortens as it accelerates: alterations from parrot to falcon, condor to kite, hawk to osprey. Omnilingual, this bird. Now omnibodied as well. Across the final reach, black vulture reverts to macaw, and at the terminal moment, the parrot veers, shirking collision. Aileron feathers spread and flatten, wingtips buzzing. The trapezoidal tail, just long enough to shelter the legs, cups to contribute drag. The parrot skids low and slow enough that its wizened head, sparing of feathers and mottled by cyst-pimpling, nearly knocks into the coder's cheek. No, nearly brushes it. The pass, a decelerated fly-by instead of a Stuka death-blow. Dyspathically intimate, this malevolent control of power. The coder cannot shift from his chine-down, belly-up abjection. Beyond the top of his head: the clickety sound of cinders crunching under taloned feet. The coder distorts his neck to see. Scarlet as before. Scarlet as always? Parrot as always? Yes. *Because living things do not change into other living things,* not outside the athenors of mythology. The parrot now approaches. No hops, no flaps. Desperate for a better view, the coder snaps his head left and right, grinding his scalp against the friable macadam. Wet hush to the stony crumblings. His head labors against a slurry. His hair: soggy with a melange of sweat and blood. He tries to raise his left arm, touch his fingertips to the moisture. Cramping stops him. Pain jiu-jitsus his defenses, spread-ing distress throughout his body. He complies with the exactions of stillness, achieves impromptu understanding of the parrot's penul-timate saltation. Of course a vulture. *Because it has located carrion.*

For expedition's sake, it declined the wonted, volant circles, the lazing down on heavy black wings. It waddles in to dine, hissing over the inert meat. Into the coder's full vision now steps the bird, unfurling another hiss. No human thew can withstand a beak that evolved to rend hazelnuts. Anon, therefore, the coder's dismantling. His only recourse: his fellow homo sapiens. Wholly absent again. The expanse of the parking lot, a disregarded moonscape, vanishes one supine body and its red oppressor. The coder, alone, watches. The parrot passes his shoulder, bobs its head at his arm, stiffens its hackles. The coder decides to bear up, whatever the consequences. He contrives a moan. Rolls. Puts his back to the bird. Neither wingbeats nor voicings ensue. The hissing ceases. Quiet caesura. Deliberation before flight? Hollow hope. Another hiss. Provocatively closer. Dares the coder not just to look but to defy. To confront with passionate hatred. He flops again onto his back. No effort required. Surrendering to gravity slumps him to his previous position. Spent. All contests renounced. As a deponent to the forthcoming barbarity, the coder squirms with incensed acquiescence. *Proceed.* The parrot could hop onto his stomach. Flapping wings could actuate a hovering search for a different landing zone. The parrot, an ace of flight, spurns the air. Favors its most awkward style of locomotion. Strolls to the coder's right ankle, where the concavity of his body dips low to the ground. Hup. Shin then knee then thigh then stops. Levers its head. Beaks the khaki flap over his zipper, tongues the weave and metal. The doubled cloth, the brass beneath, hardly deterrents, but they inspire a diffidence. Flavor could account for the equivocation. The outer brattice of cotton, perhaps offensive to the Psittaciforme palate, discourages a delving for hidden, tastier sustenances. Yet his waistline proves the objective. Where the hard, iliac crest of his pelvis gives way to the softness of his obliques, the parrot budges his shirt, exposes the underlying flesh, and tears into him, flaying off a thick strip and shaking it about. Blood spurts from the wound and showers down, splattering gore upon feathers, ratchel, and the coder's clothes and face. The bird upturns its head. Crocodilian gulp of the first portion. Cleansing swallow. Then, at the volume of its original scream, a laugh. Without opening its beak, the bird shakes with glee, taking joy in viands that presented themselves unbidden. The coder, the meal, sees his impending demise as requital for the crime of stupidity, *and feels the justice of the sentence.* The omophagic beak snaps and rips and flenses. The head dances. The gullet undulates with peristalsis from chewless englutments of dripping flesh. The coder, transfixed and aghast, watches as hot blood overspreads his midsection. The beak, splashing and slopping upon inlet and exit, derricks atop a bubbling crater. The once-white surfaces of the parrot's face, its upper mandible and nostrils and ceres and forehead: incarnadine and blending with the refulgent body plumage. The evolutionary advantage of detritivores' featherless heads, the coder understands now. His essence, which drips and sloshes: a germ-fraught risk that cranial baldness minimizes. Viruses and bacteria thrive long in the blood. Feathers can't convey the hygienic advantage of a vigorous, post-prandial shake of a bald head, nor a slear of the same against a muck-shaving surface. Standing water would multiply the gain, since baldness dunks cleaner than feathers. The parrot continues undaunted, unsatisfied, feeding with carcharodon appetite as the coder wills sepsis into its spattered eyes and mouth. He has honored his vow. He has seen. Enough and more than. To escape the pain and spectacle: his fervent wish. Loops of the ongoing atrocity: all his mental presence can provide. From defiance and grief, the coder passes into an attitude of impatience, of crazed avidity for the end to arrive. The pickaxe beak, sopping with grume, falls and rises for the umpteenth time. Insensation or death, please, *NOW!* But reality insists on the coder's attention. Into his body, the parrot now sinks its entire bust before emerging with another jiggling nosh. Somehow the coder begins to feel *less* pain. Nerves severed? Receptors blocked by trauma? He can bear no more. Gumptions himself. Lifts his head. Slams it against the blacktop.

Pain returns, but at the site of impact, not violation, where the beak splishes and gobbles. The coder cudgels his head backward again. His wakefulness, his consciousness, refuses to give way. For every bob of the parrot's head, the coder clobbers his own three times down. What he sees, feels, knows—all transudes a haze of oblivion. So long, life. Initiate hypostasis. Whiteness, then an obfuse, lukewarm radiance that exerts more pressure on his face than on his body. Shapes, colors: irresolvable. An afterlife? Bardo? Along the taproot of his atheism passes a rumble. Any glimmer of posthumous consciousness obliterates his rationalist, naturalist faith. Yet what can thinking indicate other than life? And life tells against afterlife. He has not died. He lives. And wakes. From the whiteness congeal overhead lights. The beepings of equipment intimate his presence in a hospital. He can't distinguish the human voices that enter his ears. From the hallway? From within the room? Calm voices far from the alarums and sirens of emergencies. He tries to look around. Can only shift his head to the least degree from side to side. His eyes alone provide him with greater perspective. He can feel but not move his limbs. Nor can his eyes scan wide enough, far enough, to identify anything more than the lights above. "Hello?" Him. The surrounding voices diminish, pause. Footsteps. His name. Questions from someone in the room. "Yes, I'm awake. Yes, I can understand you. Why am I tied down?" Two faces above. One male. Beardless. Almost stubbleless. Unthinkably young. One female. As unripe as her colleague. Her hair, pixied. "For your own safety." Her. "Are you doctors?" Him. "Yes." Them. The female's thick-framed glasses reduce her age further. Costume glasses a toddler dons. "How old are you?" Him. "Twenty-six." "And you?" "Same." They give their names, which the coder forgets because he does not care who they are. Cares only about his restraints. "The straps?" Him. "The condition you were in left us no choice." The male, who makes no move to release him. "You're not paralyzed." The female. "Are you aware of that?" The male. "By all means." "How?"

The female. "I tried to move. I can't, obviously, but I can still feel myself trying. Let me move. Please." "Soon enough, if we can. We have to exercise guardianship." The male. "We need to analyze your level of awareness, your condition. It's routine for us to restrain a patient until a proper diagnosis can be made. Some patients, knowingly or not, act in ways counter to their best interests." The female. "The paramedics—" "I don't remember any paramedics." "Some kids ran across you, called 9-1-1. The paramedics said you were very agitated." The male. "What *do* you remember?" The female. The coder bites himself against overinforming. "Your blood loss was significant." The male. "You couldn't tell the paramedics what happened to you. They had to get you in the ambulance fast, which required sedation and immobilization." The female. "Backboard, rolling stretcher, the works. We had to stitch you up, give you an MRI and x-rays." The male. The coder feels about to lose control of his emotions. "Am I injured apart from the wounds to my abdomen and scalp?" "No." The female. "Then *please* allow me to move. I want to call my wife." "Not so simple." The male. "Doctors, with respect, soon I'm going to start screaming. You should know this. If you don't want that to happen, take the straps off or get ready to put me under again." The doctors exchange a worried glance. "Unbind my skull. Please give me that much. My head isn't going to fly around the room and bite people." They relent. The wide strap across his forehead lifts away. To re-limber his nuchal swivel, he inches it into gingerly motions, mindful of his stitches. "As you might know, when a 9-1-1 call goes out, all three emergency services respond. Fire, ambulance, cops. The paramedics got to you first. Your ID was in your pocket. The cops did a quick search of the vicinity and found your bag by the T station." The male. "That's right. I left it behind to run." "You always jog in business-casual?" The female. "I'm losing circulation in my limbs, if you care to know. Maybe that will persuade you to remove the straps." "Your wife should be here soon. The police were able to contact her. They traced her through your ID." The female. "Did they tell her I'm all right?" "I don't see how they could have. They didn't know your condition. They only knew where you were going and that you were stable enough for transport." The male. "*We* didn't know your condition until moments ago." The female. She clears her throat. The coder can't ascertain her discomfort. "We agree that I'm all right, so, I hate to badger you about this, but, the restraints?" "We don't want to risk aggravating your injuries." The male. Too practiced at footwork, these doctors. Their choreography keeps him locked in first position. Then, zounds. The coder groks. Two doctors overseeing him because one for his body, one for his mind. The female of phrenic orientation, he'd wager. "Let's speak aloud to the issue. You think I'm *not* all right." "It's not a yes-no question. There are gradations. Doctors themselves don't always agree." The female. "Tell us what you remember about your injuries." The male. For balance, the coder slows his breathing and tries to wear a new expression. If he tergiversates into captiousness, or, worse, begins to rave and spew gibberish, involuntary sedation will follow. Will only require a needle-stick to the line already connected to his secured arms. Some version of the truth, worth chancing? "I can't give you an explanation that will make much sense. I had a good day at work. I got off the train, and I saw, of all things, a parrot. It was on the Downs fence." "A parrot? Here? In Boston? Somebody must have lost a pet." The male. "Exactly what I assumed. I tried to get closer, thinking maybe it had tags I could read. I figured it might be tame enough to stand still or even flap over to me." "Did it say anything?" The male again, now hooked. The female, not on board yet but visibly intrigued. "What happened then?" The female. "It flew away, seemingly toward the grandstand. I couldn't climb up and look over the fence, so I ran after it, flat-out. Not the best decision for a man my age, but I wanted to see if I could head it off." "Why?" The female. The coder cannot retreat. Pauses before his next steps. Determination of his mental well-being hinges on his ability to explain himself.

Doesn't know what he might have blurted to the paramedics, nor what they themselves might have relayed. "I was curious about my wind and leg strength. Again, I'm not saying what I did was a good idea. I guess I was just hoping I wasn't as old and beat-up as I feared. Lesson learned." "What about the bag you left behind?" The female. "If you look in it, you'll see nothing valuable, just non-proprietary paperwork." "Your phone was in it." The female again. "Stroke of luck that nobody stole it." Him. "So nonchalant? Most people treat their phones like treasures." The male. "I'm not most people." "If I lost my phone, I'd be freaking out." The male again. "Not to sound pompous or anything, but replacement costs aren't something I'm worried about. Also, I'm a software engineer. I encrypt all my devices such that the NSA couldn't break into them. I don't get in a twist about losing a phone every now and then. I just brick it remotely as soon as I know it's gone." He lets his story steep, convinced that news of the parrot took them by surprise. "You ran yourself almost into cardiac arrest." The male. "I have a tendency to over-commit. My wife thinks I've got a touch of OCD. Ask her when she gets here." "All of this jibes somewhat with the paramedics' report." The female. "What did they tell you?" "That you seemed to be talking about a parrot and blaming it for your wounds." "I must have been delirious." The doctors take his measure. He can tell he has appeased the male. But the female? He has only shaken her recalcitrance without disintegrating it. "Are you the surgeon who worked on me?" Him, to the male. "The very same." "Will my wounds heal properly?" "If you take care of them. You're not the first person to get injured at the Downs, by the way. They really ought to clean that place up. It's a public health hazard. They should have bulldozed it flat if they were going to let it sit for so long. Where the paramedics found you, there was an old car-stop with some rebar sticking out. You must have fallen on it, punctured yourself, then rolled onto the broken glass that got crushed into your skin." "I don't remember any of that." "Head injury, also from the fall. You have a mild concussion. We cleaned all your wounds and stitched you up lickety-split. The rebar wound was the nasty part. I think you were partially impaled for a while. Rolling off a spike explains all the tearing." The female winces at the male's description. Sanguinary injuries that unnerve the squeamish: not the bailiwick of a head-shrinker. "And it's a good thing you rolled off when you did. If your full weight had kept pressing down, you could have stuck yourself right through. Then you really would have been in trouble." "Dead?" "Hard to say, but a much tougher fix-up. As it is, you lost enough blood that we had to give you a transfusion. Also a tetanus shot. No bone damage, though, so we didn't need to call in the orthos, which is lucky for you. Those guys are knuckle-draggers." "I appreciate all your efforts. Sorry to have put you to so much trouble." "Don't mention it. That's what we're here for." The male. The coder shifts his attention to the female. Importunes with his eyes. Hasn't he ostended his reasonableness, his clearheadedness, his harmlessness to the human race? He has. She releases the straps on her side of the bed. The male does the same on his side. The coder, arms and chest freed, tries to sit up. Pain stabs him back down. "Should have warned you." The male, who hands him the controller for the bed. "Use this to sit up. Let the machine do the work. Then rotate your legs slowly to the side. For a while, it's going to be easier for you to stand or lie down than sit. The toilet isn't going to be comfortable. No showers or immersion for a couple of days. Let your body knit up some. Get by with sponge-baths. You'll have to dress the wounds daily. The nurses will show you how." The coder holds down the relevant button on the bed's controller. Folds himself upward. As instructed, he rotates his legs to the side. Lowers his feet to the floor. Poises himself to stand as his wife enters, harried. Only moments before, she would have seen him bound. My husband, the lunatic. She might already think it. Nice to know likely suspicion won't gain live consummation. She rushes to him, puts her hands on his face, his arms, not knowing how gently to touch him. "What happened?" "Do you want to tell her or should I?" Him to the doctors. "It's better if you do." The female. "The nurses will sign you out. Make sure you talk to them about the dressing." The male, who exits with his colleague. "Do I want to know?" His wife, now alone with him in the room. "You already do." She turns away. He steadies himself on his feet. "Tell me anyhow." "I saw it again. I chased it." She leans against the edge of his vacated bed. Her hands: first atop her thighs, then across her face, screening it from her husband's exigencies. Frustration, sadness, no small amount of anger in her breathy murmurings. His wife: the less-than-glowing stove burner, still singeing to touch. "Upset?" Him. "You have the gall to ask?" "I just couldn't take the quiet any longer." "I don't know what you expect me to say." "I don't expect anything. I just want to apologize. I made a snap decision that turned out terribly." "Like before." "Even worse." "Where did you see it?" "On the Downs fence. I was getting off the T. I tried to get close." "Why?" "To catch it." "Then what?" "I don't know. I honestly don't." "According to you, parrots can be dangerous." "Absolutely. Sharp beaks and claws, which is how I wound up here." He gives her his statement. "What did the doctors say to all that?" "They got a different version." "Which was?" He updates her on his revisions. "And they bought it?" "Evidently." "What about your injuries?" He relates the fall-and-rebar explanation. "Sounds reasonable." "Sure, but they don't know the truth." "Because you lied!" "They never would have believed me otherwise." "And the reasonable explanation, you don't buy it?" "I *can't* buy it because I was there." "You were banged up already. You were on the ground and in a daze. You don't think you could have imagined the rest?" He shakes his head, and his wounds cry for stillness. "What about the other times?" Her. "Those were real, too." "Before, you were willing to consider the alternative. 'I am not well.' Your words, not mine." "I revise my opinion. I *am* well. I know what happened to me. The doctors were only reacting to what I told them, which is what I had to tell them. They had me strapped down. I needed to get free." "They gave you a better explanation, *a more reasonable explanation*, and you reject it. Does that sound rational to you?" "Maybe they don't know bird-wounds when they see them." "Let's ask them." "NO!" On her face, astonishment and accomplishment. "Afraid of what they'll say?" "Clearly." "Then what does *that* tell you?" "I can't be the only man ever attacked by a parrot." "No? I hereby designate you a single-case anomaly. And what do we do with anomalies?" "We discard them if we can't repeat them." "See any way to repeat this?" "Thankfully, no." "And what happens after the discard?" "We go with the most impartial extrapolation from the data." "Which is?" "What the doctors said." "Paydirt." "Except they're wrong." Professional and well-trained, all the brains and hands that have attended him. His mind, more highly wrought than ever for ways to confer the reality of his experience. "No one else has seen your parrot, let alone touched or been touched by it." "You can't say that." "Someone else *has* seen it?" "Possibly. We just don't know." "If it's alive and at large, somebody else would have reported it by now. We'd know. We'd have heard." "How?" "The internet! Signs on lamp posts! Flyers! Word of mouth! Telegrams! Something! *You almost died*, so now you need to say where we go from here, because, me, I'm at a loss." What he has told her: how the parrot ripped into his midsection. What he has not told her: what he did when he couldn't tolerate another moment of torture. He holds in reserve the wherefores of the bandages around his head. "There might be another theory." Him. "For what?" "The whole thing, first-sighting up to now. It's not something I took very seriously until today." "Out with it." "It's in what you said. *My* parrot. *My*. That's the key. It's after me, no one else. That's why I'm the only one who has seen it. It waits to get me alone." "And why would it do that?" "The molecule." "You don't smoke it anymore, or so you say." "That's not a lie. I don't. But I smoked it regularly for years." "'Flashbacks don't apply.' Again, your words, not mine. Were you wrong?" Grave and roped to her, he collects himself for an arduous ascent. He'll point from the peak of the scabrous barricade and hope she sees what he sees. "I wasn't wrong. The parrot isn't a flashback, and it's not a hallucination either." "What is it, then?" "A messenger." "From where?" "The dome. The beings." Her face goes blank, then cracks apart with laughter. She rolls her hands at her wrists. "Keep going. I've got to hear more of this." "I've visited them. The beings. Now they're visiting me." "The beings *and* the parrot were at the Downs?" "No, just the parrot. The beings are visiting it *on* me." "Why? How?" "All these years, I've thought of the molecule as a me-to-them portal, but maybe it also works the other way." "But you've only seen them in there, not out here." "Correct. Out here, only the parrot." "I'm sure you have a theory about that." "It's their emissary." She closes her eyes, and he believes that when she opens them again, she will step into the hallway, keep going, leave him behind, and never return. Instead, she moves toward the wall and sits on the floor, elbows atop knees, head drooping. "Their emissary." "So I theorize." "What's this emissary's message?" "I don't know." "And why an emissary instead of the beings themselves?" "I don't know." "And the most important question, why did this emissary attack you?" "I don't know." Each avowal, softer than its predecessor. "None of this makes any sense on any level." Her. "I agree." Their last exchange before a nurse knocks on the door and edges it open. "Folks?" "Come right in. The asylum never closes." His wife, still on the floor. "Ma'am?" "Don't mind me. I'm just drained. Being married to a nutcase can do that to you." "Don't I know it." The nurse, who tutors them on sanitizing his wounds, monitory against the temptations of rest. "Don't lie around all day. Walk, move, gradually build up. The body isn't meant to stay still. And don't worry about your stitches. They'll hold." The coder feigns normalcy, almost wishes for the old practice of keeping patients overnight for observation. Those days, long gone. He can stand, sit, dodder, vocalize his needs, clean and toilet himself. GTFO: the medical system's ukase to anyone in his condition, pain notwithstanding. The nurse departs. "We need to leave." His wife. In the hall, she commandeers an empty wheelchair and rolls her husband toward the capacious elevator, which opens and closes, starts and stops, with velvety softness. No free-clinic, this hospital, as the stubs of his insurance premiums attest. The atrium, a hangar of glass. Outside, the air of the hilltop hospital degusts of the freedom he almost lost. The coder tries to cover his joy, inappropriate for exhibition, yet his wife, so long his partner, must know his emotions as he knows hers. She wants solace from him. He wants to give it to her. Owes it to her. Can't clear the debt. Can't even make a minimum payment. Tapped out, his resources, and at the worst time, when he has bled her of goodwill. From him, a judicious, quiet interregnum. After the chaos, look for the calm. The drive home presents an opportunity to consider in silence what has happened and what might happen still. She maneuvers him down a mild grade toward the parking garage. Finding the car, finalizing the contortions required to evulse him from the wheelchair and lade him into the passenger seat: distractions from the tension. She refunds the wheelchair to the lobby while he waits. Not acknowledging him when she returns, she keys the ignition and backs from the space. Slow-squeaks the tires on the garage's polished tarmac. Inserts her paper ticket and credit card into the payment station. Drives under the boom barrier striped in yellow and black. An anfractuous ramp ushers them onto the roads, ordinarily hellways, but now inexplicably quiescent along the route they travel. Inscrutable and mercurial, the local traffic deities, sowing mayhem on the main feeders to the turnpike, the interstates, the tunnels. The coder and his wife roll beneath an overpass. Above, the unexceptional condition of gridlock. More or less the twenty-four-hour case except for an ill-defined midday window when an invisible thrombolytic wafts through the air and dissolves stoppages. Boston: ever an hour from Boston. But his wife doesn't comment on the eerie frictionlessness of the drive. Her silence feels willful, aggressive. The coder wants her to speak to him. They gain the neighborhood. The fence around the Downs. The T station. The Mont rises just ahead. From the passenger seat, the coder stares at a red light and tries to will it to green. Each second stretches. His wife wants him to wallow in shame and defeat. In negativity. Why else drive up the front side of the Mont and not the back, with its detente-establishing panorama of the ocean? Her decision, to grate him against all that has mangled him, then rub his snout in the sludge. Leastways the abasement doesn't last long. They reach the house. She parks in classic Mont style, half on and half off the low-curbed sidewalk, a straddling imposed by the pre-automobile narrowness of the streets. His wife, unencumbered by sutures, makes a fluid exit of the car. She leaves him to extricate himself, strides into the house, closes the front door. The coder, abandoned? Knows not quite. Feels so. Could do with some handholding and body-leaning to undergird his diminished powers. Has to move. Can't stay in the car all night. Tries to move. Profound muscle stiffness despite the ride's brevity. Reaches for the handle of the door. Pain. Pulls. Pain. Opens the door. Pain. Trundles his right leg onto the sidewalk. Pain. Klaxons of the body's vulnerabilities. Breakage auguring breakage auguring death. Reminds him of how a tweaked back turns the smallest movements into tai chi dolorations barbiturately paced. And among descriptions of his injuries, the word minor cannot appear. As the body-man said: almost right through, the depth of his gouging. The coder scoots his nates to the edge of the seat. Lifts himself clear with the assistance of both hands on the top rail of the open car door. Feats that prompt a running cascade of almost intolerable pain. Only after he reseals the car and stills himself, standing, rallying strength, does the cascade ephemerally taper. If his molecule-craftsman can synthesize lidocaine, the coder might have to place an order and self-administer. He imagines his wife walking in on him mid-injection. Graduation to mainlined heroin, she'd posit. He snorts at the idea, and core muscular contractions pierce him. After a long series of foot shufflings, his only bearable technique of transit, he reaches the stoop. Tries the front door. Locked. Keyless, he must knock. Silence for a minute, maybe two. Knocks again. He can't believe she'd banish him for the night or longer in his condition, prevent even his children from admitting him, but perhaps he has overtaxed her tensility. Finally, the door opens. At the handle, his daughter. Chary steps pilot him to the kitchen, where the house's flattest, hardest surfaces accommodate his tribunal. His simmering wife, seated between his children. His son, a portrait of twitchy discomfiture. His daughter, phizzed with sadness and fear. The coder cannot sit. Too much pain. Can only stand and await. The central figure folds her hands, either from depletion of rage or rage redoubled. Six expectant eyes upon him. "Dad." "Dad." "Tell them. Everything." He accedes, but requests a temporary stay on medical-hardship grounds. Grudgingly granted. The committee's exhaustion redounds to his favor. Mercy enables the members' quick retreat. With difficulty, the coder settles onto the couch. Too punishing to climb the stairs. Purposeless in addition, for pain will keep him from elongated rest. He hopes to kidnap from wakefulness a brace of naps, build from those toward restoration. The next day arrives. Perhaps he slept before his wife comes to help him up. He relives the enervations of rising from the hospital bed, of entering and exiting the car. Does not apply a thermocouple to his wife's wrath. Presumably it has cooled, else she would not have assisted him at all. He takes her hand and pulls gently, rising as she ballasts him. Once atop his legs, he can manage a slow self-reliance. To the bathroom, headmost. Afterward to the kitchen, where someone, either his wife or one of his children, has fixed him cereal, still dry. Carton of milk sweating beside the bowl. "Thanks to whoever put this out for me." Him, to the vicinity. "Team effort. Your son got the bowl, your daughter the milk and cereal. I told them to leave it dry since we didn't know how long you'd be in the bathroom." "Avoidance of soggy cereal. I couldn't have asked for more." "Make sure you don't." Before disappearing for school, his children deliver him his laptop and phone. His wife says goodbye as she leaves. No kiss. Not much eye contact either. Suffices. Knows he deserves far worse. Munches cereal. Emails headquarters. Relates the minimum. Homebound. Unfortunate accident. Touch-and-go for a few hours but now patched and mending. Will soon return to the office. Until then, will work from home. Fields a smattering of get-wells. Not many. People too busy, responding to emails only on an emergency basis. The get-wellers might gripe about him. Faking ill health. More likely, no one at the office cares all that much, and won't if he bears up productivity-wise. Atop the kitchen counter and from thick books, he fashions a pedestal, places his computer on it. Codes. An anodyne, to excel. Doesn't kill his pain. Only smothers its loudest decibels. His promise to his family clogs the chambers of his mind, and he never pretends that work will excuse him from confessing. Nor can his divulgence wait upon the full remediation of his wounds. Soon, soon: his subtext as he parries his wife's admonitions. He wants to remain capable of movement and speech through an open-ended grilling. Two months of abeyances prepare him. He will not have to dive in medias res for a recess. He calls everyone to the kitchen. Bids them sit around the table. Speeds in review over what they already know. Facts aplenty, including the doctors' anagogies of his grisly impairment, have seasoned the previous weeks. "But there's another version. My version. Your mother knows it. You don't, but in a few minutes, you will." He crash-courses his children on the molecule. Chronicles his history with it, how he has used it in his work. Postulates how it might relate to the two times he has returned under third-party care to the house. He spills all he can about the dome, the beings, what they do, and the parrot as their suppositional messenger. Pauses in response to questions. Clarifies and expands where possible. Ends by underlining his longstanding sobriety. "You told the doctors all this?" His son. "Not about the molecule, no." "Why not?" His daughter. "They had me tied down. If I'd told them what I just told you, I doubt they would've discharged me." "And what about the parrot?" His son again. "I told them I saw *a* parrot and that for fun I tried to catch up with it. Doing that while being old and out of shape accounted for the condition they found me in." "You told them the parrot attacked you?" His daughter. "No. I thought they'd never let me go if I said what I saw, what I experienced." "Mom?" His son. "This is your father's story. So far it's the same as what he told me after the doctors were out of earshot." His wife passes a consoling hand across the boy's back. "Tell me again what the doctors think happened to you." His daughter. He recapitulates. "They didn't go looking for another theory because I gave them one that fit." "But how can this be?" His daughter. "Dad—what?" His son. "I can only say what I saw, what I did, what happened. I can only report what my senses reported to me. And I'm telling you, I was clear in the mind. My decisions maybe were terrible, but—" "Maybe?" His wife. "I misspoke. My decisions were terrible, but that doesn't change what I saw and experienced. My senses were fully functional. They were not in any way—" "Deranged." His daughter. "Yes." "And yet." His wife. "And yet." Him. "What's the simplest explanation?" His daughter. "That the parrot is a hallucination. That I've been smoking the molecule and worse for years and have been lying to you the whole time. But does anyone believe that? If you think so, say so. I won't be angry." No accusers. "What's the second simplest?" His son. "Brain tumor." His wife. "Ruled that out." Him. "Third?" His son again. "Mental illness." Him. "What does your therapist say about that?" His daughter. "She's not into labels. She's more of an advice-giver about what I should or shouldn't do. I should've ignored the parrot. It didn't come after me. I went after it." "Aren't there medications for something like this?" His daughter again. "Psychoactive meds are a dead end because all of them have hallucinations as side effects. And I can't emphasize this enough: the parrot is not a hallucination." "What do you think, Mom?" His son. "I think your father has gone 'round the bend. I think the parrot isn't real. People don't need to be high or tumor-ridden to have hallucinations. I think his overactive mind has cocked this bird up from nothing. That's why no one else has seen it. I also think he's going to get himself killed chasing it. Why he wants to do that is another question." "I don't agree with your mother's take." "Which means we're where?" His daughter. "Where we are." Him. "Can't you just ask it what it wants? Parrots talk, right?" His son. "I'd love to, but I haven't had the chance. I'm not even sure this parrot talks. Mostly what I've heard it do is scream, remember? The whispered scream it hit me with was one of the reasons I went looking for it the night the policewoman brought me back here." "What were the other reasons?" His daughter again. "To see. To verify." "IT'S NOT REAL!" His wife, who springs up and paces but doesn't leave the room. "Why didn't you do what your therapist said you should do?" His son. "I don't have a good answer for that. I gave in to a compulsion." "The next time you see it, are you going to wig out again?" His daughter. "I'd like to say no, but based on my record, I can't." "Maybe there won't be a next time." His son. "I considered that, but I rejected it." "Why?" His son again. "Understand, it's just a hypothesis." "Dad, quit stalling." His daughter. "I'm not stalling. I'm just not comfortable with what I'm about to say, even though it makes some sense to me. You've been asking what I should or shouldn't have done, what I might or might not do, but I'm not sure any of that matters anymore. The attack was methodical and directed at *me*, you understand?" "No. None of us do." His wife. "I'm talking about the facets of the unknown. Why this messenger? Why this message, whatever it is? And why give it to me? And why now? I've borne down on all these issues." "And concluded what?" His wife. "That I might have worn out my welcome." "Mom's not throwing you out. Wait, *are* you, Mom?" His daughter. "No, not just yet." "You're not following me. Worn out my welcome *in there*. I didn't mean to, but I did." "With the beings?" His son. "Yes." His wife sighs. "They worry about manners?" His son again. "I don't know if manners is the right way to put it." He looks at his children. For a teen and pre-teen, this discussion? "Words are failing me, kiddos. Just trust me that not only is the molecule not for children, it's not for most adults either." "You said that already." His daughter. "It bears repeating." His wife. "But you haven't been back since you last smoked. Why bother to sic a bouncer on you now? If anything, you threw yourself out. You think they're pissed about that?" His daughter. "Not about that, no. I think they're pissed about what I did all the times I was with them." "You said they were always thrilled to see you." His wife. "They were. The vast majority. I ignored the dissenters because positivity was by far the norm. The dome comes and goes so quickly that you can't waste time if you want to get anything done. You've got to focus. That's what I did." "Focus on what?" His son. "On what you go in for." "Which is?" His daughter. "Information. Of a sort. I'd go in confused and come out wised up. The problem I couldn't solve, I'd solve afterward in a matter of days, sometimes hours. I think that's what they're pissed about—how often I used them to get myself unstuck. I never gave them anything in return." "Like what?" His daughter. "I have no idea. But it seems as though I've stiffed them, and now it's time for me to pay." "Do you hear yourself?" His wife. "Yes. Spirit-animal malarkey. That's what I'd call it if someone else were saying it." "I married a rationalist, atheist, empiricist scientist. Tell me where he went." "He's standing right here." "Why would they wait so long to collect?" His daughter. "I can't say for sure, but think about the hospital bills I racked up recently. It'll be months before they all go out. Think about how long court cases take. Sometimes years or even decades. And that's us. Humans. That's the slow grinding of our institutions. Who knows how things work with the beings? Maybe slow for us is fast for them." His wife stands staring into the empty, adjacent room. His daughter inspects her mother. The coder, appalled to have brought everyone to such a pass, feels untold gratitude and sympathy for his family. "You say it's real. Mom says it's not. Are we supposed to pick who's right?" His son, meaning himself and his sister. "I'd never put you in that position." "You already did." His wife. "I suppose that's true." "Solve the problem for us." His wife again. "I can't." "Super." "There might be a way." His daughter, whose parents look to her for clarity. "You have to ask it what it wants." "But I can't find it." "Not out here. In there." His wife throws her hands up in disbelief. His son's eyes probe and wait. His daughter, an analyst of impressive candlepower. Fatherly pride swells in his heart. In another context, he'd post her up for a high-five, for she has lifted an edge of the shroud. He ponders the wisdom of crawling under. "Out here, you almost died. Now your daughter tells you to go back in, and you think it's a good idea?" "But that's the rub, isn't it? I can't assume I'm any safer out here than in there. I don't know if it's a good idea, but it's our *only* idea." "Gotta do something. This is something. Do it. Behold your father, children, the megabrain." "What do you think?" "Do not ask your son. He does not get to decide." "I'm asking him to weigh in, not decide." "I don't know, Dad. My answer is, I don't know." The coder looks his family over and sees three people sucked dry, knows a mirror would display a fourth. "I move to adjourn. I think everyone has had enough. I can keep going if you want to, but I'm pretty wiped out. At the same time, you don't have to wait for us to reconvene to ask me questions. Come and talk to me whenever you want. I'll do what I did here, try to give you the best explanation I can. Also, I promise not to do anything without consulting everybody. In the meantime, there's nothing to worry about." "There is if it comes back." His daughter. Her subjunctive hangs, but no one swings at it. Deliberation abates for weeks. The coder heals to where he feels irked by the standard pangs and smartings of all men his age. And as his body recedes, his mind advances. He codes and cogitates. At night, before bed, their children safe in their own rooms, he and his wife trade monosyllables about the topic over which open wrangling has not resumed. "Don't." Her. "I think I have to." "No, you don't. And what I mean is, I'm scared." "Me, too." "Then, why? It could be gone for good. Can't you wait it out?" "I don't want to, not if I don't have to. This has got to stop. All of it has got to stop. If there's a way for me to end it, I've got to try." "I can't say yes, but I won't say no." "Why?" "It won't stop you. And I won't speak up just to get stomped. If you go, you go with my hopes, not my nod." What will he choose if his kids echo her? His children: subordinates who might have derived from their creativity a sense of power they do not possess. Not in charge, those two. Will he have to veto them, the progenitors of ideas he plans to exploit? Cloture soon, whether the minors yea or nay it. And if he re-enters, how will he find and ask? Intradome communications don't reconcile with standard interrogatory structures. The notion of communication itself slips away. Not once has the molecule furnished him with straightforward interactions. More soulforce-to-soulforce bonds, covalencies of numinous vibrations. The beings as vengeful loan sharks, the parrot as their enforcer. He has staked himself to this theory. The flames lick at his soles. Unreciprocation, hypothetically his crime. How to make restitution? And a thought he has not mentioned to his family: suppose his malfeasance flows from simple trespass, from having dared to enter an inviolable zone. And not just once. Over and over and over. The temerity of another encroachment. An ultracompounding factor. Then the knotty quandary of turf. All his clashes transpired here, in the outer world, not in the other/inner/nether/para world. And his foregoing defeats: circa mortal, even with home-field advantage. In media impetus at the Downs, he despaired before the parrot's constraint-breaking powers, the same powers which, for all he knows, will transform into deific omnipotence throughout the infinite, evanescent territory of this polymorphous, polyphonic magus bird. Forward or turn away. Interface or retreat. As binarisms arise from his subconscious, he forces them under again. Too suggestive of agency. His approaches and actions feel semiautonomous in retrospect. Surrendered his reason. Should have retained it. Might not then have blundered. Endeavors now to proceed with more care. In the dome, no chaperone. Should matters disintegrate, he might also, returning whole-of-body yet sieved-of-mind. His fear: salved by anterior trips, escalated by what he has already undergone. Unreckonable risks at each stage of the project: re-entry, prowl, collision, inquest, flight, extrication, appraisal, and actuarial calculation of sanctuary in the quotidian forevermore. Leap and leap again. To think on this, to think hard on the how of it, he repairs to his study. The door closed but not locked, opens after a knock. "What are you doing?" His son. "Thinking." "Not working?" "No, just thinking." "About the molecule?" "Yes." The coder looks at his son's face, takes it in his hands, feels the lissome, tender, stubble-less skin. The boy bridles under his father's cradling. "Dad." "How often do I do something like this?" "Never. That's why it's weird." The coder releases him. The boy: watchful, unmoving. "Try not to think of it as a drug. Think of it as a transportation device." "Like a car?" "Yes, in the sense that a car takes you from one place to another. No, in the sense that wherever you go in a car, it's familiar." "What if I've never been there before?" "Doesn't matter. You'll see people, plants, the road, the sky. All familiar. But that's not how it is with the molecule." "Where does it take you?" "I don't know, even though I've been there many times." "Is it far away?" "It feels far away, but I don't know in what direction." "But it's real?" "As real as you and me talking to each other right now." His wife calls them to dinner. They look at the open door but don't move. "And you didn't pay them back?" "This is my hypothesis." "But how would you even do that?" "I don't know. I'm hoping to find out. Maybe they'll tell me, or maybe they'll somehow know I'm sorry, not just for what I did but for not realizing what I was doing. Maybe they'll see I learned the lesson they were trying to teach me, and that'll be enough." "I don't understand." "Neither do I." Unsettling, the boy's mien of worried calm. The coder does not look away. "Are you scared?" His son. "Yes." "Were you before?" "The first time or two, I was leery, but my curiosity won out. Pretty soon I was excited to go in again." "Why?" "Because even though I never knew what I was going to experience, I knew it would be positive." "But not anymore." "No." "Because of the parrot." "Yes." His wife appears in the doorway. "Did you ever go, Mom?" "Where?" "Where Dad goes." "Only once. It wasn't for me." "How come?" "Let your father answer that." "I don't want to put words in your mouth." "Go ahead. I'll weigh in if need be." "Historically, there haven't been many enthusiasts." "There must have been some." "Yes, but the blast of it is what puts most people off. It's like being shot out of a cannon twice: once to enter, once to eject. It's very jarring." "Mom?" "That's an acceptable description of why I didn't like it. Now go wash up for dinner." She points him out the door and closes it. Gone before the coder can gauge his mood. Peeved? Let down? Frightened by his mother's intervention? Pacified by information already assimilated? The coder's wife, contra uncertainty: irate yet contained and more threatening for the pressure. "Why'd you get rid of him? He was asking good questions." "When you smoke the molecule, will you still be here?" "What do you mean?" "Just answer." "My body will be here. My mind won't." "What'll that look like?" "Like me lying down." "Like you're dead?" "No. I'll be breathing the whole time. I might even shift around a little." "Like you're dying?" "You know the answer. What's with these questions?" "Our son asked me them earlier today. I could tell he was about to ask you." "Why didn't you let him?" "I was afraid of what you'd say." "How did you answer?" "Pretty much how you just did." "Then why didn't you let me keep going?" "Because of what comes next. 'Are you going to die?' Go." The coder hesitates. "And there it is." "I don't even get a second to think?" "Not when it's our son we're talking about. But go ahead, now that you've had time." "Based on past experience, there's no reason to think I'll die." "And how do you think that'll sound to a child?" "Like the truth, which is what you told me to tell." "And what's the truth-value of scaring your son?" "He's already scared. We all are. But the fact remains, going back in is the only workable plan." "What about changing your therapist, switching from psychology to psychiatry?" "Now you want me to take drugs?" "Different drugs." "We've been through this. Side effects are why we opted against psychiatry in the first place." "Who opted?" "I opted. You agreed." "Now I'm disagreeing. We tried one way. It didn't work. Try the other." "Why? We still wouldn't be able to tell side effects from principal effects. If I swallow what a psychiatrist gives me, I won't know what to expect. I have no way to tell normal from abnormal. Not seeing the parrot wouldn't prove anything either, since I hardly ever see it. On the other hand, I'm practiced with the molecule. Because I've got some notion of what's coming, I've got some chance of control. I won't be totally subject to the unknown. Every drug is a megalopolis. New meds would just rob me of my map, my GPS, and my ability to speak the language." "But you don't speak it. And you've lost the map. And your GPS is on the fritz. You go back in now, you're going in weaker. You're not in control. You, this, *everything* has gone nuts. You have taken leave, dear husband. And I knew—I knew!—all those years ago when I tried that stuff that something like this was going to happen someday." He doesn't challenge her, but baloney, what she knew. She only knew what he did: that the molecule worked for him and not for her. Neither of them could have forecast the current imbroglio. "A stone face? That's what you've got for me?" "I'm thinking." "Think about this. If what you suspect is true, the people, beings, entities, whatever, are going to be angry." "Maybe fuming. But I can't let that stop me." "Think about how much you owe them. Think about your net worth. Think about your family. This house. Everything you've got. Couldn't they say they gave you your life? Maybe now they want it back." This variant, he'd not spied. Forces him to pause. Wrenches the events at the Downs. Not a harassment operation completed. An assassination interrupted. He compiles his thoughts. "You're still going to do it, aren't you? You *want* to go back. I didn't realize it until just now." "I want to get this resolved." She slams the door as she leaves the room. He forgives the cliché because he prefers it to getting punched. Passing days temper the animosity that the conversation with his son, the argument with his wife, engendered. The coder refrains from fidgeting, pacing, nail-biting. Motionlessness whenever possible. Seated with optimal posture. Deep breaths. Gather the faculties. Heightened emotion cannot underprop a launchpad. He must ground the environment to elude calamity. Explains as much to his family when they convene to decide his time of departure. Informs them that he has listened to and weighed their concerns and objections. He feels he must persevere. Asks them to act as Earth-based command posts. Attempts levity with a walkie-talkie imitation. "*Krrrkh*. Houston. Come in, Houston. *Krrrkh*." "*Krrrkh*. Ground control to Dad. I read you. *Krrrkh*." His son. "Me, too." His daughter. "Glad for the buy-in from the next generation. Let's hope for a united team." He expects his wife to shun him, but her eyes meet his and lock. "I know how important it is for you to go in with the right mindset, so for the purposes of unanimity, I'm supportive, but let's get on with it." He leads them into his ritual, beginning with the coveralls, sets of which he distributes to everyone. "Do we really need these?" His son. "Yes, and you still might have to burn the clothes you're wearing." Him. "Once you get a whiff of this stuff, you'll understand." His wife. "The liftoff platform doesn't smell great either." Him, as he directs them outside to the garbage shed. "My loge and lazarette." "Dad, you've got to be kidding." His daughter. "It conceals the stench, and it's not somewhere you'd be inclined to go poking around. Now you know why I'm always scrupulous about the lids being on tight." "You said that was for rats and raccoons." His son. "It is, but it's also about making sure nothing spills when I have to move the cans to lie down. Voilà." He takes the rolled blanket from the lintel. "Wouldn't it be better to sit or squat? Or kneel?" His daughter. "It's best to lie down. You'll see why when I launch. Calm is all. You need steadiness to set the machine aside without dropping it. You also need to be able to rest your limbs. The blanket is my cushion, plus my insulation in cold weather." "It stinks in here, Dad." His son. "Smells better than the burning molecule." Him. "How can that be?" His daughter. "Just wait." His wife. "Help me pull the cans out. There needs to be room inside for all of us." Him. "Out here is good enough." His wife again. "I'd rather be in the shed, Mom. These coveralls make us look like spacemen. At least if we're in the shed, no one can see us. So embarrassing." His daughter, agrasp of a handle, scraping the can onto the landing. His son and his wife, last but in deference, follow suit. "Now what?" His son. "Normally I wait for an empty house before I even get started. It feels strange to have opened up the whole ceremony." "Strange-good or strange-bad?" His wife can't conceal her genuine concern. Does not on a fundamental level wish him ill. Wants everything to go well, for him and for her. For everyone *through* him. "Strange-good. Comforting to operate in the light instead of the dark." "All the times you came out here in coveralls, didn't the neighbors ask what was going on?" His daughter. "Who's to say they ever saw? Look how far below the main sidewalk we are. And what's to see? Just a guy in coveralls in his garbage shed. At worst, I'm a germaphobe, which is run-of-the-mill in this country." Above, cloudless. Humidity, negligible. Loved ones, fully informed about history, crossroads, intentions, hopes. Never such an impediment-free flightline for takeoff and landing. He unveils the machine in the guise of its two major components. "I've kept these under the kitchen sink forever." "That's where you stashed them?" His wife. "Sure. When was the last time you went behind the garbage disposal?" "I'm not the one you should have worried about." "Kids, have you ever seen this stuff before?" They shake their heads. "And if you had, what would you have seen?" "An old wine bottle." His daughter. "A glass tube and some steel wool." His son. "Id est, junk. Except unbeknownst to you, purposeful junk." From one pocket, he removes a torch-style lighter. From another, a screw-top pill container, the domicile of his supply. To illustrate, he holds out the bottle. "Into the neck, the wool. Onto the wool, the waxum. Then you heat the neck until the waxum melts and distributes itself through the wool." "There's no smoke." His daughter. "There shouldn't be. Not yet. That'd be a sign you're overheating it." Him, as he sets the machine down and unrolls the blanket, sits cross-legged on it, takes up the machine again, plugs the mouthpiece into the punt. His trio packs in around him. "Mind if we pinch our noses?" His daughter. "Go right ahead." Him. "This is weird." His son. "The weirdest." Him again. "For the record, I don't like what's going on here." His wife, head bent, kneeling on a gardening pad she has lifted from the slatting. "The fact that you're all with me, it means everything." Him. "What happens next?" His daughter. "I'm going to load the machine by turning the bottle upside down and heating the wool. Smoke will start pooling in the chamber. Technically, it's not smoke because the molecule is vaporizing instead of burning, but you get the idea. When the chamber is full, I'm going to exhale as hard as I can, emptying my lungs. Then I'm going to inhale likewise through the mouthpiece and hold as long as possible. I'll exhale again, and that'll be the first hit. Then I'll do two more hits, and once I begin, I won't speak." "Why?" His son. "Words are anchors. They hold us down, so it would be best if none of you say anything to me after I start. Perhaps you'll see my eyes open briefly, perhaps not. I try to keep them closed as much as possible. After the third hit, I'm going to hand the machine to one of you and lie down." "Won't it be hot?" His daughter. "Warm, not hot. Even if you hold it by the neck, it won't burn you, but take it by the barrel just to be safe. While I'm lying down, I might shake like I'm having a mild seizure. Nothing dramatic. Don't be scared. It's just the molecule doing its work. Maybe think of me as moving around in my sleep. And that's it. I'll be back soon, one way or the other." "How long will it take?" His daughter. "Tricky question. For you, a few minutes. For me? Notions of time and space rather disappear, along with everything else." With his eyes, he polls for remaining issues, but he has cleared the agenda. "Good luck." His son. The coder suppresses an urge to enfold them all. Saves it for afterward as something to anticipate, something to lead him back to the standard realm. "Everybody ready? Watch how." He fleets into the rocambolesque fauvist intensities he has entered so many times before. The neon palettes in crisp geometries that dazzle and transfix and overwhelm him—how can he pioneer this measureless tremendum? He drops into the oneiric calyx of the vapor as all distinctions egress from the workaday. No fear yet added to the fear he has long nurtured, but the breeding colors soon dim in luminosity, brindle and fade in luxuriance. And lo. Cachexia throughout. The intercalated, sempiternal frameworks of the dome jettison their integuments and disaggregate. He does not feel tenanted in a flosculating network of lightstone dolmens that harmonize with spacetime. Instead, a deluge of acid burns through his pith. Blame for this apocalyptic washing away, of himself along with the molecule's polyprismatic variegations, somehow rests with him. Replacing the heterogeneity that erstwhile prevailed? Nullity in a continuum effaced of heart and grief and joy and music and tears. The un-humanness of the Plank seconds subsequent to the nativity of the universe. Terror inundates him. Overfills him. He metamorphoses into a jactitating vessel of awestruck horror, detonates into a googolplex of annihilating photons—each containing a him more dread-aggrieved than its brethren, each bound to its replicant by a light-spring of limitless ductility—that disperses and re-condenses only to re-explode immediately in recursions beyond number. Mind-yowl. Heart-shriek. Spirit-wail. Echt Gehenna. Not a myth. He has lit upon it. Will now writhe interminably. This sterility: the contrary of purity, simplicity, goodness, sinlessness. He transmutes into a quintessence of unassuageable rue, dies an octillion anguished deaths in each rendition of non-time anew. Ghastly neutrality, bleached and ashen, incinerates and re-constitutes him as a pinioned, keening umbra. Then, an effusion supplants the blanched nothingness. Ethereal and murderous in hemoglobic, ineluctable shades, a numen moves at superluminal velocity to engulf him in a phagocytic process. The immanence! The throes! Revelatory of death's amaranthine perdurance. Anamnesis of all dejection as every chroma perforates him. From this trial, no mode of life can return, for the harrowing will never slacken. The coder looses a soundless howl not for life but for a less love-riving death. Ages ago, not moments, he succumbed to suffering that has always lasted and always will. Selfsame certainty, as waverless as his suffering. Inane to speculate on the bathymetry of his torment. Preposterous to sound it. Fathomless, fathomless. Until a vacuole opens and rises. Levitates less a shade of clemency than an infinitesimal rift in the unbounded painscape, a semiquaver of silence in the triturating thunder. However long passes. Sets of rogue-wave agonies stack themselves across galactic fetches, boom and tear through him before the vacuole reappears and parthenogenesizes. The parrot's septic, carmine brume-nature curdles. Foam before froth: the decomposition of the molecule's sway, its eternities yielding to mundane temporalities. Patches of wellbeing gnaw at the murk, superseding vermilion contumacy, and the coder thumps to violent berth, his soul a dusty burlap sack flung with contempt back into his body. He sits up, tremulous from toes to hair. "Dad." His son. "Dad." His daughter. "Say something if you can." His wife. "It's me. I see you. I'm back. It's over. It's worn off." He touches his wife on the arm, his children on their cheeks. "That was fast. Nine minutes. I timed it." His son. "I told you it doesn't last long." "It didn't feel fast." His daughter. "It sure didn't." His wife. "How was I? Did I do anything, say anything?" Bombshell content-from-without might aid an unriddling. "Nothing really." His daughter. "You looked like you were sleeping." His son. "Okay. Good." "Disappointed?" His wife. "I wouldn't say that." Prevaricator. Done to death on cliff-bottom rocks, his aspiration for rapid sensicality. "What went on in there, I've never experienced before. I was hoping you guys saw me do something that could help me unscramble it." "The trip, was it good or bad?" His daughter. No amount of hyperbolic teenage cynicism can mask what presents itself to him: her guilelessness when questing for information. Still a child. And hallelujah. He won't hurry to mature her with an exegesis on ineffable despond. Waits and waits, searching for verbiage befitting the question. Her brother, more tyro, less patient, can't stand the delay. "Did you find the parrot? Did you see it?" "I made contact with it." "Did it speak?" His daughter. "Not with words. It never has." "What did it do?" His wife. From him, a wry visage. Please, think hard. You've traveled, only once, but one trip supplies enough in-country acumen to remember you can't come plain-dealingly back from where everything jacklegs and ramifies. "It didn't do anything, per se. Things don't do things where it is, not in the usual sense." "That's not what you told us before." His son. "No, but there's no guarantee of consistency. If the molecule teaches you anything, it's to be prepared to be astonished. To always be open to astonishment might be a better way of putting it." "Were you astonished?" His wife. "I can't even tell you how much." "In a good or bad way?" His wife again. "Did it do anything *to* you?" His daughter, sapping another mine. Replaces the one he sidestepped. Deft, this daughter of his. Makes him proud and afraid. Wishes for his son to emulate her. Wishes also to remain present and able to savor their development. Futile to dodge again. "Yes." They file from the garbage shed. Strip off their coveralls. Throw them in a can. Replace the lid. Push the cans back into the shed. Close the doors on his launchpad, now denuded in perpetuity. His trunk balances uneasily atop dithering legs. He leads his family to the steps. Expects to gain the sidewalk.

Gains only one stair before his legs permit no further exertion. Turns and sits down to three concerned faces. "I thought I'd shaken it off. Give me a minute or two." "Is this normal?" His daughter. "No." Him. "What happened?" His wife. He institutes a wits-gathering for the imminent effort. Words: the projectiles most easily repelled by the molecule. Onward withal. Into the travail. "I think it showed itself to me. It found me and showed me what it is, what it can do." "Did it know you were coming?" His son. "I had the feeling that as soon as I arrived, it knew. It was already there, waiting for me. I believe it has always been there, that *there* is its basic nature." "What about the beings?" His daughter. "No sign of them. It seems to me now that it, the parrot, the expression of it I just experienced, superintends that world, or *sub*tends it. Everything there falls within its power, which is plenary. I think it wanted me to feel its supremacy." "Dad, what are you talking about?" His son. "I'm sorry. I know this can't be making much sense." "Kids, go in the house, please. I'd like to talk to your father alone." With a flick of her head, his wife quells any protest. The offspring heed and disappear. The coder, jittery hands clasped and hanging in the air between his knees, awaits questions he can't answer, yet he would never impugn his wife's entitlement to ask them. "Bad trip." Her. "I've had bad trips before. This wasn't that. I don't know what this was. I still can't believe I made it back. Seeing you and the kids again feels miraculous. I'm waiting for my body to re-acclimate." "The dose you took seemed pretty heroic. Maybe it was too much." He appreciates her plain tone. Not a time for scolding, nor feckless recrimination. Later, if ever. For now, an assessment, then a groping toward a plan. "I did it the same as every time. Same set, setting, and amount as always. The only thing different was that you guys were watching me." "You think that was the problem?" "No. I liked that part. I liked not having to hide. It should have eased the trip." "Even given what you went in for?" "Now you're getting at it. Intentionality. It's a killer." "But how could you have avoided it?"

"Couldn't have. Try not to think of a purple cow. You can't do it, not after I say it. Same with this. I wanted to find the parrot. I went in with an objective." "Don't you always?" "Not like today." "Show me your hands again." Steadier though still unquiet. "What was it like?" "Terror, sadness, desolation, all of them wrapped together times a trillion." "Did you learn anything?" "How to feel pain beyond pain." "Anything useful. Anything to guide us." Recollection stirs vertigo until his wife moves bodily into his visual field. Waves her hands. Snaps her fingers before his eyes. "You're sure you're back?" For a blip, he feels estranged from her face, but the hiccough elapses. With caution, he stands up, fingers splayed, arms low and held away from his body. Wants to ensure equilibrium, which might yet shift. The stratum beneath his feet: stable. Legs conjointly. Fortitude now for the staircase. Step over step, and up. "Don't rush it." Her. "I feel fine now. No more wobbliness." On the sidewalk, he executes a hop-in-place, lands in a paused lunge. Jazz hands. "Ta-da." "Goofing around isn't going to make this better." He straightens. Paces five squares uphill on the sidewalk, undoes them downhill. Specimen-like before his wife. She scouts him from a blind of vegetation and wattle. Did she remember waterproof ink and rainpaper pages? He freezes, the natural reaction of a mammal under study. "It's not fun being ob-served." "It's not fun being the observer." "You're waiting to see if I behave normally, but that doesn't happen under a glare. You snap the klieg lights on, and people bunge up." She unlocks. Turns away. Looks downhill. Covers her face with her hands. Cries. Embraces him when he hurries to her. Weeps into his chest. Phrases of consolation effervesce and rupture before he can speak them. Vacuous all. To lend them voice would not comfort her. Would stoke her upheaval, not to mention his own. Where he has davered with his family: into some chasm. Its walls: photoconsumptive. Its ceiling: overbending and self-welding in fontanelle style. He holds her. She heaves and shakes. As her sobs downshift and peter, he does not pull away, nor she from him. He longs for an extended lull. The deepest intimacy with his wife in months. Accompanied yet, even now, in the wake of the juggernaut. "We should go back inside." Him. "And tell the kids what?" "That I'm all right. It's true." "For the time being." "Maybe the tribulation I just went through will act as a safeguard." "How do you figure?" "The score has been posted. Me: zero. The parrot: a billion. I forfeit. This was my last journey ever. Perhaps I never should have gone, but I did, and I got the starkest warning." "I thought you said what happened at the Downs—" "This was way worse. Sobriety from here on out. It's not the catchiest saying, but I'll get a tattoo of it if you want." From her, a harrumph in which he hears more solidarity than scorn. She backs away from him. Clears her eyes of tears. "It's not really a plan." Her. "Tomorrow's going to be a normal day. So will the day after that and the day after that and all the rest. Done and done. I got the message." "Let's hope so." Soon a relapse of his night terrors. And when they awaken his wife, she snarls in groggy tones about the substance at issue. Dispenses, in dribs of bile over the course of weeks, her long-harbored and self-censored hatred of the molecule. Midway through the night or in the still-dark hours of early morning: her time of spavined disburdening about the too-high price from the outset. Flattering, her credulity that even if he hadn't dabbled, his achievements and fortune would have burgeoned regardless. He does not agree. The molecule gave him an edge. In tech, in business, no slow-and-steady lane. First place or get shot. She knows his opinion. He leaves her the full stage to stride with sibilant harangues. She claims she pressed on him with great vehemence the molecule's danger: that it scourged trifling. He upends his memories. No caveats skitter out. Which doesn't contravene her case. Monomaniacal, his frame of mind back then. The molecule: the philosopher stone of legend. He had to tap it, drink from its wellspring. He'd pledged his allegiance solely to that which aided him, and if his wife did indeed warn him, he never would have assented to her advice. Confides his error. "I don't want you to feel guilty for not hindering me." "Guilt isn't what I'm feeling." "Anger." "Yes." "I promise—" "Don't promise. Just get yourself together. No more risk-taking." He swears to obey, but at his next therapy session, he does something he has not done before. He lies. By omission: leaves out that he partook again of the molecule. And by commission: avers that his wife agrees with his decision to reduce the frequency of his visits. The psychologist: fluent at the friezes and stirrings of attention. Two fingers to her lips. Ruminative positionings of her head. Crossed legs with phalanges interlaced and demure over her abdomen. One palm against her cheek, the other cupping her elbow. An expedient straightening of her glasses. An inhale as preparation for curated speech. "I'm surprised to hear you're thinking of cutting back, considering your recent experiences." Her, versed in his Downs misadventures. "Not that recent. My injuries are healed." "They were very serious. I'd even say gruesome." "And my own fault. But I've learned from my mistakes." Each lie greases the excretion of its successor. "I feel on an even keel these days. I also think I'm starting to repeat myself in here." "Repetition can highlight patterns. Speaking of which: the parrot?" "Neither hide nor hair of it, or perhaps I should say neither feather nor beak." "And more generally with your wife?" "It's great to be on the same page with her again." "That's a loving reaction, it seems to me. What do you make of it?" "Only that I wish I wasn't also sandbagging it, meaning that I've had some insomnia again. My wife has started sleeping in the spare room." At his feet: the crevasse he has pried open. "Joint decision or unilateral?" "She brought it up, but I'd been thinking she might want to decamp. She can't sleep with all my fuss. Who could? I should have suggested it first, though. *That* would have been loving." "Why didn't you?" "Too chicken. I didn't want her to go." "And when she suggested it, what did you say?" "That absolutely she should go. People have to sleep. She could barely get up for work." "How's she doing after making the change?" "Back to normal, such as it is."

"And you?" "Funny thing. If nobody wakes me up, sometimes I sleep right through, no matter how much I'm flouncing. Sometimes I even wake up feeling rested." "And your work?" "Fertile and profitable." She prods him to describe the Downs incident. "Again?" "I want to make sure we didn't miss anything. It's a precursory technique, also a de-sensitizing one." "You're checking to see if I can keep my story straight." "Not exactly." "But roughly." "Consistency is something we have to pay attention to." "And haven't I been consistent?" "Remarkably." "Indicating what?" "That's a question for you to answer." "Significance. Truth-telling. Reality." "Those sure sound like answers to me. Have you noticed any change in your emotional response?" "To what?" "The experience, as you've recounted it and re-recounted it." "Less anxiety." "That's good. How about obsessive thoughts?" "No. None." The basso profondo of his lies! He misleads in wavelengths too long for her to register. Through all of his falsifying, he holds eye contact. Not a hint that she doubts him. Why would she? He neither premeditates nor palters. Merely speaks in Voltairean style, concealing his thoughts rather than revealing them. He cannot detach from his last dalliance with the parrot, the whorling efflux that permeated him, that held him catatonic for excruciating dissolution. Revisit and revisit: aftermath's imperative. Just what he ought to explore in therapy. Yet an irresistible drag restrains him. By contrast, his facility for work? Aggrandized. Each line of code unspools itself into a thread he binds to others, weaving software fabrics of splendid luxuriance. He can't not see that his vagabondage through the hellscape resulted in an upjump of his virtuosity. Involuntarily. *Contra*voluntarily. Wanted only to elucidate the parrot's petition and comply with it, if he could. Wrong, wrong, wrong, everything he believed about his dome-interactions, for his pandemonious ordeal rhymed not at all with past practice, and his enhancement followed nonetheless. Visitation alone must produce the effect. This insight slews him from dicey equilibrium into volatility. His experiment never could have mollified the parrot. Could only have enraged it. His trip, not down Golgotha but *up*. Haled to the severest woe, and haled by himself. And what he knows, he does not betray. He erects a firewall. Ordains himself on one side. Unchurches his family on the other. No information will pass through to rimple the flimsy, quadrilateral truce. But the remand from crisis cannot last. Fact One: the advancing maelstrom will devour his wife and children. Fact Two: even oblique contact will liquidate them. His task? To deflect the wickedness. As before? As always? He continues the spoor of normalcy. Doubles down on commuting. Goes to the office almost daily unless he must retrieve a car from the shop or admit a tradesman into the house. His wife's eyes train for longer periods directly on his own. Wordless, empathy's machinery and exertions. Emotion to emotion. His wife becalmed leads to him becalmed, a trend that propagates to their children. Rounds of school and friendships and athletics and extracurriculars turn and turn again. Placidity without. Teeming within. Of thoughts and projects and stratagems and schemas. Away, away from the menace that looms! He deconstrues quietude as dormancy and keeps on with his family-preserving incubations. The rain falls, contendeth the evangelist, on the upright and unjust alike. Debatable, contendeth the coder, for any archaisms dawdling in the present deserve ruthless examination. We audit nature to the ninth decimal place in quantumelectrodynamic precision, yet we refuse to molt the personified supernatural. Animism and magic: philosophies catering to human narcissism while the universe points always toward indifference. To defuse potential acrimony between his analyses and intuition, he slips his outlook through a not-yet. The parrot along with the dome and its inhabitants: natural entities *not yet* catalogued and ratiocinated by science. Molecule-related websites crepitate with testimonials slantwise duplicative of his own. Replete, the evidence, though anecdotal. The coder will build out his hypothesis and place it under fitting academic strain should he succeed in weathering the approaching phase. To what he knows, he adds what he feels: the facinority nearing itself to him every day, if it doesn't surround him invisibly already. In the Boston damps of October through April: destruction just avoided. The veneer of atmosphere through which the moon shines? The mists that turn stoplights into trichrome blemishes? Not condensed and gelid water vapor. The parrot nebulous in disguise. Or rather, the parrot out of disguise and stalking as an exterminating frowst. Having spotted the masquerade, having identified the amorphism that hazards him, the coder guards against innovative modalities of attack. His sudden wheelings, his sustained glowerings into any sky sashed with clouds, elicit puzzlement from coworkers. Stopping why? Looking at what? Such behaviors, if not backed by reason, fall beyond the jurisdiction of sophrosyne, and the coder's newfound penchant for scowling at a block of ostensibly empty space enters the annals of his tics already on file at the office. His nth bypassable idiosyncrasy, adjudge the parametric lords of profit and loss. Greenlit to indulge at will, as he does and must. The outdoor-indoor dyad, its danger-safety oscillation, fosters in him a scurrying mindset. From the house to the car. From the car to the T. From the station to the office, where he hunkers and from where only the most bothersome and rare group-exhortations can jimmy him. Celebrations materialize at the securing of a patent, the attainment of a stock price. Wise on these occasions to conform. Truckling cuts down on hectoring and questioning. Groups operate always and everywhere to shield individuals from perlustration. Outside, the coder adheres to the largest nearby faction of conspecifics. Fears any cranny the parrot might surge from. Worms toward the group's center, cosseted by the herd. Indoors again, talk the small talk and thereby deploy volubility to break the manifest form of stranded and vulnerable quarry. Strong with the pack. An illusion workable enough, but these successes, these months of pedestrian vanquishments? No event in the last twenty-five hundred years cajoles him to doubt the Heraclitean dictate. Panta rhei. Everything flows. Before the stream turns, he must decide his stance, the where and how of it, and soon, for beneath his feet, a caldera heats and pressurizes at the parrot's behest. Completes a peerless environ of jeopardy. Abscond. Sidetrack the impending eruption, the tempestuous downflow of pyroclasm. He will die inhumed by it. Others needn't. And die not the molecule's simulation of death. The thing itself, with a competent professional poised above his collapsed body, if his body remains existent and assembled. Two fingers pressed to his radial artery, then to his carotid to establish the paralysis of his heart. An ear and cheek lowered also to his buccal cavity. Yes, lungs, too, zed. Accompaniments to his final trajection? The rattles and squeaks of a gurney. The rustle after the long zip of a cadaver pouch. His discoverer, if already acquainted with decedents, will call an undertaker. If callow, an ambulance. Alerted by this thought, the coder houses at all times upon his person his do-not-resuscitate form. His body, withheld from the ground and furnace long enough for the transplant surgeons and medical students to butcher out their morsels, fleshly and abstract. Better that than embalming, yet another ghoulish American practice born in war and stretchered into peace and now too profitable to consign to the smoke and abattoir of statecraft. His guiding ethic anent his death? Only me, not them. He can't save himself. Can only save them. Has only a chance to save them. As primary game, he can attract death, draw it into a detour. Hope to sate it such that it won't reconnoiter for second, third, and fourth helpings. Tenacity: the sword he draws from its scabbard. He must disembroil those dear to him. He must go. Not a self-exfiltration piqued by fear, though he would never deny his fright. Rather a decoy action galvanized by love. Of his motivation, the coder need not convince the parrot. Tempt and nudge it only. His gamble obliges a concomitant obsession on the imbalance of forces. The parrot: immortal, pervasive, unscrupulous, unrelenting, faceless, disembodied, and moving at the speed of light. The coder: mortal, local, plagued by guilt and indecision and anticipatory regret, identifiable, naked to all the misfortunes of languishing flesh, and creeping at the speed of people. Thermonuclear warhead against a balsa hut, this contest. All the more reason for the coder not to swerve from determination. Over his lunch hours, he calls and emails his lawyer, his financial advisor, his agents for health, transportation, home, and life insurance. Six distinct and hardy creatures who reassure him of ironclad paperwork. The coder lets on nothing to his wife about his flurrying correspondence. Due diligence he should have performed before the family huddle in the garbage shed. Fiduciary malpractice on his part that he procrastinated. Lost to him, the luxury of unpredictability as to the timing of his death. Now, plain fact, in the near future, a coderless world. He must quadruple-check with assiduity the correct inscription of every glyph and ligature in every contract and policy entering into force upon his quietus. Poring through these documents jabs him to the precipice and leans him far over it, well-nigh horizontal and face-down. Bound still to life only by an attachment of his toes to the brink and the parrot's illegible caprice. He internalizes the fact that amoral-at-best institutions cradle his loved ones' futures, and the reams of legalese almost falter him. The welfare of his family: dependent on corporations. Scumbag buckraking entities. He knows from having spawned his own. Can taxonimize their ingredients down to every share of common stock. And insurance, to cover and protect? Dedicated to the opposite. To *abjuring* coverage. To *withholding* protection. He imagines raging from limbo as companies balk on disbursements contractually obligated. "What did I pay all my premiums for?" Him, in a revenant's cry. "To enrich us and impoverish you. Welcome to capitalism." Him again, with the phronesis gained from fortune-building. Long ago, he surveyed the massifs of his funds, hoping to feel shielded and feeling only imperiled. Now replay. His insurance policies: training manuals for twerp MBAs. Instructions on depicting peripheral commas as tripping lips for deadfall clauses. The repercussions? His family destitute and shorn of redress. Cataclysm might unfold. Dystopian scenarios enchant his mind as he contemplates every bleak phantasm. Bankruptcy. Homelessness. Unmitigated banjaxment. Inspires a vision of his family crouched naked and unsheltered on a hail-bashed prairie. The grave endangerment innate to his plan. But graver endangerment if he abdicates. He forswears the elixir of affirmation. Clinches to the point of unendurability the depravity of his vanishing. Provokes rounds of auto-rejoindering, claims and anti-claims, until at last the cross-checking ends. Months of tranquility, of hushing routine. All deceived but him as he presses on with reinforcing the bulwarks. Total commitment for everyone, beknownst or un. The facts he has amassed? Lightsticks he cracks in half and sweeps together. Plunges his hands into the rickle. Shakes both loaded fists. Pushes forward what he grasps. Cotyledonal fluorescence hums low, then builds. The crescendo: paltry. The darkness ahead: illimitable. The light he emits: farcical, mingy lumens. He nevertheless grubbles forward, the sole direction. He chooses roads over runways. Must subvert the ease of tracking him by air. Would have chymed and absorbed the digitized intricacies of airline security had he known his life would someday twist into the contours of a runagate's. Outstripped by events. To fly under an alias, he would have to purchase identifications exquisitely counterfeited. The sequelae of any minuscule flaw? Arrest. The parading of his duplicity. His forced retention in Suffolk County Jail. Nashua Street. Just south-bank riverside before the harbor. Too-close vicinity to his loved ones on the Mont. He could not place his faith in the vouchings of black-market forgers. Smarter to wheel away. On the fateful morning, he needs a pretext for taking his car to work instead of the T. "I got wrapped up with a long podcast. I want to finish it on my commute." "Use my headphones if you lost yours." His wife. In her hand, a nest of wire. "I didn't lose mine. It's just that I have to crank the volume because of all the extraneous noise on the T, and I wind up with a headache. The planes have been driving me nuts lately, too." This last claim, any Mont resident can make and never rouse debate. "The planes I can't help you with. We're stuck with them as long as we live here." "It's not just the T and the planes. Too many people also play their devices at top volume, no headphones. Reminds me of the old boombox days." "What does?" His daughter, yawning herself into the conversation as she comes down the stairs. Still heavy, her eyelids. Still clad for sleep, her fledging body. "Your father was talking about how people turn their phones up in public." "I hate that. What's for breakfast?" "You're old enough to make something for yourself." His wife. "Lame." His daughter. "Where's your brother?" Him. His daughter flaps a vague hand toward the stairs. "In my own car, I can control my environment. That's the nub of it." Him, surmounting the hurdle. His wife withdraws her headphones. "Suit yourself, but don't complain tonight about how bad the traffic was." The boy appears, rubbing his eyes. The coder takes in the sight of them all. Blind fortune dictates that none of them face him when heartache nearly fells him. Steady. Wipe data from faceplate. Refresh with complaisance. For them, all for them, his inevasible piacular rites. He must compartmentalize his emotions and effectuate his maneuvers—predominant: exiting the house—before remorse dissolves the bulkheads and floods the ship entire. Redolence dandles his nostrils as pancakes crackle on the stovetop. Eggs and milk from the fridge. Fork from the drawer. Box of mix from the cupboards. His daughter has collected the instruments, embarked on the quartet. In order to lubricate his actions, the coder clings to the reverie that he stands amid a normal morning and will see these people again only hours from now. "I'm off." No response from his wife nor from the boy, whose head, hair cattywampus, lies atop an arm outstretched on the kitchen island. "Bye, Dad." His daughter. He turns from them. He must slice the graphene tether that holds him back. The bounty of self-deception? Indepletable, fortunately, for every step toward the front door requires him to gorge and gorge. The rending surplus he crams into his gut—he has closed the front door behind him—nauseates him so greatly that two blocks downhill at the base of the Mont, he pulls to the curb, folds himself over, and gasps his queasiness into repose. His wife explodes into his mind. She drives this same route. She could pass and see him paused. Could wonder and investigate. "Dropped phone." Him, rehearsing an excuse. Allots himself two minutes to recover. Cannot weaken. Cannot concede, neither to regret nor fear nor psychosomatic ailment. Bests himself by thirty seconds. Straightens up. Checks his mirrors, which give back nothing of note. He rolls toward the task. Drives past the left to the tunnel, takes the left at the next light, then u-turns and darts into the self-storage center where, months ago, he covertly rented a locker the size of a walk-in closet. With cash and a fake ID—buying one for this purpose sat calmly with him—he pre-paid for a year. No hurry. Still inchoate, the plan and its timing at the moment of rental. Obtain a space, stock it with generalities. Canned food, clothing for warm and cold weather, batteries, books, a tent and cookstove of some kind, a supply of hygiene products, a hand-cranked lantern and radio. Refine the stock as research and time direct. His machinations placed him among fringe company: motley survivalists, whose online guides he rummaged for benchmarks and gubbins. In his typical manner, the coder bought all the books, though shipped them to his office. Left work early on days of his choosing. Schlepped the books on ride-shares to the storage facility. Read. Then walked home after another ride-share to the Mont station. Coordinated all these peregrinations to coincide with his normal stroll-in time. His storage space acquired pulmonary dynamics as, over the progressing months, his books and gear accrued and eroded. Enlightening, how tinned and dried foodstuffs can almost supply the plenitude of a balanced diet. Sardines, lentils, powdered eggs, and sun-dried or canned tomatoes alone cover ninety percent of the fulfillment. Fresh vegetables: the only staple not susceptible to unrefrigerated transport. Vitamins in pill form intercede for leafy greens. At the start of his groundwork, he considered but rejected buying an RV. Not for him a lumbering vehicle. Celerity needed for the upcoming turmoil. With room to spare, his sedan fits a month's worth of non-perishable protein and high-fiber carbs. Water? Potable and plentiful at just about any off-ramp, but for supplemental insurance against contaminated sources, he stocked a trove of purification tablets. Chlorine, chlorine dioxide, and iodine: how he'll slake himself from rivers and creeks. His prospective endpoint? Wyoming. The least populous state. By hundreds of thousands of souls, even less-peopled than Alaska. The coder recalls from pre-digital days the aspect of Wyoming on a paper map. Indian reservations in axolotl pink. National forests in baize green. In Wyoming, loneliness and climate take turns scything the weak. There he will entice eradication, his own and the parrot's, atop a remote butte or mesa, a private Armageddon on par with the theorized kosher correlative, Tel Megiddo in northern Israel. For the transposition, he covets wastelands scrubbed of life more advanced than sagebrush and insects and lizards. But first, the load-up of his car. And before that, the seclusion of his storage space, wherein he sits upon a laden tote and weeps. Tears already building as he drove from the Mont to the facility. Wondered about his ability to steer if he began to sob openly. No place to pull over. Three lanes of traffic snailing along. Vehicles so close together that interstitial air functioned as couplings. If he'd had to stop mid-slog, he would have targeted himself for road rage, Boston-style, best-case scenario involving an assailant pounding on his window and hurling racial epithets until horns honked for retreat. He has witnessed the custom before, each time amazed that the target didn't reply with gunfire. Which the coder never would, but still. Preventative self-care, his temporary hold on his lacrimal glands. At the storage facility, he even remembers to snatch from the glovebox a microfiber cloth. Secreted in his locker, he presses the shammy to his face. Nevermore will he see all those he loves! He blubbers, yet stanches his tears before they equate to a time-sink. Events advance. He can guide them or knuckle under. *Follow me.* Him, in icy telepathy to the parrot. Stands up. Wipes tears from his face. Lugs bins to his car. Locks the storage space behind him. Three hours since he left the house. Time ravaging itself into a gullet that expands and expands. Incognizable, the capacity for all previous intake and the unending to follow. His pre-payment of rent will expire months from now, and his wife, perhaps by then past sadness and bewilderment and well into hatred of him for his abandonment, might root through his mendacity to the storage space. Unclear whether she could gain access. He didn't write her name on the paperwork as a licit entrant. His leavings? Auctioned if she can't obtain the correct documents in time. The remains of his storage space could mimic his corporeal ones: scattered, untraceable. He will die far from the range of human eyes. Might end up outright vaporized. Or something near to it. Repels as a sentimental contingency the urge to write a note, seal it in an envelope, leave it behind. Him, the parrot, the high plains of the west. He must orchestrate the decrement of complications as a final antecedent to oblivion there, deliverance here. Done with grieving. Done with packing. On with driving. Time to roar out and finish with doing and living and forlorning. With a fast hairpin right, he zips onto the jugum above the commuter-rail line, swerving right again to join the feeder road to the tunnel and the pike. Fortuitous, the three hours he expended. Rush hour has dissipated. His plan launches itself through Boston's window of least congestion. What a pleasure, what a release, to ramp up and feel confident of sustaining speed. More the Boston choices: zoom and stop short, or crawl and stop short. Southwest, his direction. Toward the overpasses, into the tunnel, under the river, then to bisect the city. West of Worcester, no traffic will qualify as traffic. Boston has jaded him too thoroughly to apply the word too liberally. Retroceding: the Mont and Winthrop. Then Chelsea. Then East Boston. The roadway lifts upon its piers. Exhilaration! Soon the tunnel. Under and through. He passes signs for Logan airport and its off-ramps, signs for the Sumner Tunnel and the Williams, toward which he accelerates. Until the last bend before the mouth. Stomps the breaks. Zugzwang! *Traffic! STYMIED!* Dead stop. He blares. Grips the wheel. Torques it with such force that the plastic yelps. In the rear-view mirror, vehicles clot the artery. Incalculable exposures to this very circumstance in this very location, where four lanes pinch to two, have taught him to vacate hopes of forward movement. Minutes pass and give way not even to an inching. Noisome smog accretes to an anvil-shaped thunderhead above the pavement. Rooted vehicles add an upper layer of steel to all the concrete uniting the horizons. He opens his door. Stands on the sill. Gawps toward the maw of the tunnel, back at its constipation. Mercy, Boston! His phone? Still in his pocket. Has received no texts since his departure from the house. Orthodox, as he has yet provided no one with cause to worry. He plans to dispose of his phone in the nearest body of water he can reach with a lob from his speeding car. Guided by a paper road atlas and person-to-person artisanality from there on out. But now, here, he consults the oracle. His traffic apps: worm farms of burning red. Local news sites, no help either. This lockup, too fresh. Old lockups, too scadded. The inescapable, inherent shortcoming of boundless searchability? Everything appears and nothing stands out. He tries the radio. Insipid commercials and bombastic right-wing rumormongering. Other drivers exit their cars. Pace. Smoke. Kibitz with their fellow prisoners. "Anyone know?" Him, rhetorically to the throng. Outlandish and loathsome, this jam. Future generations will tell of it and tremble. Agitation forces him into laps around his car, first walking, then jogging. Two revolutions at the faster clip actuate dizziness. He increases the diameter of his makeshift track. Ragged.

More a lumpy, closed perimeter than a loop. He dekes around conveyances of all sizes and shapes before returning to his own. "Hey, boss, stick by your car. We might start moving." Someone. "Let him run. We'll be here til doomsday." Someone else. Sweat and heightened breath duopolize his biology. He brushes this fender, that bumper. "Get it, Gump!" Another someone, farther distant. The coder's convolutions expand. He flirts with, then crosses, the shadow of the tunnel's mouth. The lighted teeth of the architecture's maxillae could bite down and encage him for gnashing. He jukes back into sunlight. From this part of the jam, no cheers, no scoffs. Precious few people exterior to their vehicles. Bemusement from drivers and passengers as he trots by. Faces pry from screens. The phones of the quickest-reflexed track his movements. *Filmed.* Agape at his blindsight. Smartphone ubiquity tricked him into carelessness. Might already have torpedoed his plan. His family! What they'll see of him! He needs more time to draw out the blast radius. With luck, the phones have captured only his passing, not yet his face. Dorsal videos of him, unrecognizable. Of no interest. Delete upon reception. And by moving faster, he might surprise each driver into a too-delayed response. Into the tunnel, he speeds himself duly. Exhaust sours his mouth and throat. Scorches his eyes. Blackens his lungs as horns skronk. People stand about in knots. "Hey, guy!" "Is he the owner?" "Great. Now this clown, too." "The cops'll catch him." "The cops couldn't catch a cold." "We're gonna be stuck forever." He soon passes an open window, driver seated, yakking at her phone. The coder overhears six words. "Red. Went right by. I swear." Almost stops him. *In the tunnel?* At the nadir of the shaft, a crowd spans the total width of the bore. Wadged around what? About to learn by barreling forth. Enough heads turn. Enough hands tap enough shoulders. Enough fingers point. Enough phones rise and flash. Proximate, the outing of his behavior, whereupon everyone he strove to save will die. He couldn't have stayed in the car and done nothing—temporarily?

Days might have passed before his wife contacted the authorities. She would have called the office. No sightings of him reported, but the conjecture? Holed up somewhere with an idea, dissecting it. She would have boiled at his absence, but she would have waited before clanging alarms. Yet now, the plan in rubble. Smashed by another capitulation to impulse. *And the parrot foresaw his weakness.* Still moving, the coder grazes a side-view mirror, and his gait decays to a stagger. His delusion that he can wrestle all parrot-related happenings into rational sensibility, a delusion that he now for the first time apprehends definitively as such, scuds about his head in microscopic adhesive droplets he can't throw off. He flings only beads of sweat to either side. With the backs of his hands, he squeegees away salt, still nearing himself to the crowd. Fell fiasco, his decision to exit the car. Accepts the onus. Knows he has blown the project in toto. Stillborn in the phase-zero trial, and his fault moreover. His actions proved unequal to his stratagems. Final appetence: to redeem himself through battle. He hoped only to behold his own and the parrot's undoing, but because of his failure, all will now behold their own in addition. The crowd, having seen and begun filming him from a distance, breaks open a gateway. He avoids collision. Continues on. Unblinking eyes burn his clothes away, then his skin. The air cools him, pilfering heats of vaporization from his bared musculature. He gets clear of the crowd, and not far along the graywacke: the monstrous bird, its head nearly at the height of his shoulders. Beyond, police cruisers in a line across the tunnel. First responders and the debris of an accident should strew the surroundings. The sheerest luck that traffic stopped without a pileup. The police hope for containment until capture. No other explanation fits. He stops and looks around. Realizes that everyone sees what he sees. One must, after all, see to record, and this truism plows into him with the force of an epiphany. Documented! Stamped as present in reality! *Now to remove it therefrom.* Behind him: the backed-off crowd and the jutting vanguard of chariots. Ahead: the police and their cruisers. Above: the whooshing ventilation system. The tunnel echoes with the horns of frustrated drivers. The coder, transfixed and sweating, bends at the hips, palms on knees. Voices yell to him. He registers sound, not sense. Can't waste neural activity on parsing fripperies. All of his attention on the bird. It clicks its talons, puffs its feathers. These mock-charge theatrics gird the coder's heart. The parrot, *afraid.* It turns toward the line of police, back toward the stopped vehicles and the crowd, then squares itself to the coder again, unable to divine a safe direction. The parrot's evident fear: invigorating, for with each heave of the coder's breath, equilibrium and the promise of greater strength draw near. The parrot expands. Its blood-red plumage blazes. Its feet and claws: stout and deadly, a dragon's rugose, megalodactylous armaments. And about its shoulders, the sculpted, steroidal density of pit bulls and gorillas. As the head turns, filaments of spittle drag and stretch and break and fall from the beak, whetted and glistening with slaver. The coder does not flinch from the parrot's radical enlargement. He has watched it change species in real-time, mid-flight. Revision to greater size can't tax its proficiencies, nor the coder's capacity for dumbfoundment. But what now? All assembled wait. None can fore-tell. Who or what will initiate? The why-here and why-now elements of the bird's appearance speedily cohere: to intercept him at the least-escapable place. But the parrot's unambiguous distress proves its miscalculation. Proves also its subjection to fate. Victimized by destiny, just like the coder himself! Demigod at best, this bird. Its mortality sweeps revenge into the bounds of the feasible. The coder's hands curve into fists. His sharp nails dig into his flesh. He shows pugnacious incisors. Resigned to death, on his way to abet it, he dives into faith. Noise and the waving arms of the police: the last stimuli his mind assimilates before he seizes upon the bird. The texture of fabric. Solidity beneath. Not the airiness of layered feathers. Surpris-ing, but all and all the least deviations the parrot has ever exhibited.

The coder, undeterred, locks with his hands and teeth. Rends with the first. Rips with the second. The mouth-feel of hair. His tongue and palate wash with briny, mucilaginous, extrinsic blood, since an errant bite teaches all tongued creatures the flavor of their own. His ardency for a sabred gob! For a constrictor's mandible to spread wide and engulf his prey! He shoves the serrating blade of his face into gore. The near-evisceration that the parrot once inflicted on him, he now endeavors to repay. The bird counterattacks, soundtracking its savagery with barking and snarling and growling, evidently believing in canine vocalizations as potent coder-repellent. Another miscalculation. Yet the beak sunders him wherever it finds flesh to mutilate. The coder's pain: slight compared to his racking in the parrot's world, but worse by orders of magnitude than his violations at the Downs. Here, as there, the bird shreds his flesh, but here, unlike there, it also splinters his bones. Audibly. In multiple fractures and snaps. The schisming reaches him even through the screams he vents into the ruptured avian body he continues to destroy. The beak crushes and demolishes with the slamming impacts of a broad and toothy snout. It vises upon his torso. His ribs pop and crack from a front-to-back pincering. This pulverizing beak of industrial hydraulics—*he will end the bird that owns it*. But he cannot eclipse the assault on his thorax. The beak flattens his lungs, and, vacuumed of breath, the coder champs his last, hoping through the suffocating daymare that by tearing a final portion from the bird, he will overthrow it biologically, metaphysically, omnipresently, utterly, and for all time. The autopiloting of his consciousness through gristle and meat: what he farewells as he wisps into the void. The sequent stagnancy and blinding whiteness, he recognizes from the aftermath of the Downs. He tries to cry out. Cannot. Emits instead the hoarse cough of an antique bagpipe. Clarion enough to call his wife to his side. Does not see her approach. She appears holus-bolus above him. The binding across his forehead, more restrictive than its precedent. Perhaps his record has sold him out, motivating the doctors to tighten all straps. "Don't try to speak. They had you ventilated. Only whisper if you can." His wife, assaying him with visual scattershots. Her hair: pulled back in a hurry. Locks coddiwomple free of the band, antennae undulating for indications. Her face: haggard. Either ten years have passed since he last saw her or his antics have aged her a decade in—how long? She reaches for him, onsetting with tears. Her fingertips stop shy of his cheeks. "Please touch. I'm not a bubble. I won't pop. I need to feel you." Him, rasping. She, his yokemate, takes his face in her hands. She lays her head on his encasted chest. Sobs drumbeat her and intensify his pulse. Alive. This incontrovertible fact feels past belief and also unwelcome, for if he lives, what of his antagonist? He suspected much of the bird, but never that he could kill it and survive. "I'm in the hospital." "Yes." "What kind of hospital?" "The same as before." "Where?" "The same, like I said." "No, what wing?" "ICU. You've been unconscious for days." "A coma?" "Chemically induced at first. Then they withdrew the medication and hoped you'd come back on your own." "How many days?" "Four." "And from here, where are they going to put me?" She turns her head to meet his eyes. He tries to pet her hair. Muscles engage to no effect. "I can't move anything." "Everything that's not in a cast is bandaged or sutured or screwed together or otherwise immobilized. I'm surprised you can blink without pain." "When I'm healed, will I be able to move?" "Just get better first." "You misunderstand. Will I be *permitted* to move?" She cries for a time more. Nerves yawping, he tries to comfort her. Gives up. Joins her instead. When their jags wane, she lifts her head, touches the moisture she leaked onto his chest. "How bad is it?" Him. She strokes his harnessed hand. "Much better now that you're awake and talking. When you came in, the doctors—" "I can imagine." "No, you can't. That's the thing. You can't." "They didn't think I was going to make it?" "They said that if you could get off the ventilator and back to consciousness, that'd be huge. And here you are." "Except I don't feel huge." "How *do* you feel?" "Weary. Pinned down." "They've got you doped up. Can't be surprised by that." "Thankful is what I am." His eyelids droop. "Do you remember?" Her. Only every second until blackout. Him, silently. Knows the wisdom of holding back details until safe passage declares itself. "I remember a big traffic jam." "What about your car?" "I remember getting out of it." "Do you remember how you packed it?" His eyes take in the bag attached to him from a tall tower. Readouts scroll on a rolling monitor near his bed. "I remember getting out of the car to kill time." His wife does not look away from him, does not repeat the question he skirts. His gratitude draws sustenance from her compassion. In his condition, he could not uphold consciousness through an argument. Conflict would drop him into a self-preserving sleep. "What are they saying happened? What did I do?" He knows what he did. Wants, though, to hear her speak of the malignancy he extirpated. The eyes and devices that recorded him: instruments of instantaneous, worldwide ratification. She won't now deny his probity. "You attacked a dog. And no schnauzer either. A great dane." Her answer so starkly contrarizes what he expected to hear that he cannot admit it for intellection. The constituent words: rough-cast phonemic marbles thrown against his comprehension. "They said you might not remember because of the trauma." "I don't remember a dog." He has never told a truer truth. "Maybe not, but blankness isn't your forte. I know you remember something. You don't have to tell me now. Actually, I don't want you to." "I remember red." "That was the shirt the dog was wearing." More marbles, which this time shatter. "The owners were tourists. They had their dog in a baseball jersey. On their way home, the dog escaped. They were driving, going through a slow section, when one of their kids rolled down a window. The dog jumped out." "At the pinch point in the tunnel." "That's what caused the traffic jam. The cops were trying to remedy the situation when you showed up." "A dog." "Say it as many times as you want. It's not going to make it false." "I thought I saw—" Her eyes scald him. Her masseters bulge in her clamping jaw. "Do not say what you saw. We both know what you saw, but I've told you what it was *in reality.*" "This dog—" "You tore into it with your bare hands and teeth. We need to sit with that. Let's be calm. Let's be happy you're conscious again. Let's not ask for more, not *say* more, in your case. In a minute or two, they're going to notice I'm talking to you, not just waiting here in another vigil. That's when they'll rush in to do their evaluations. Watch what you tell them." "I remember from last time." "Good. Get ready for an encore." Her tidings? Not possible. He saw. He felt. The parrot. No other. Deceived by superficial form, his wife and all her corroborators. "What happened to the dog?" "The police had to shoot it. They might have got you, too, but you weren't moving. In the ambulance, you had no pulse for a couple of minutes. They brought you back with a defibrillator." As nurses move into the room and signal for his wife to leave, the coder mulls an image of himself between shock-paddles. Dead, and officially so. "I'll be right outside." His wife, as she exits. He has not seen his children. Hopes that in his condition they have not seen him. Knows that they must have, visiting either at his bed rail or from the other side of the glass. He projects himself toward the ceiling, looks down at his plight, cannot bear the thought of speaking to his children from within his wounds and bonds, not without an explanation they'll accept, which doesn't exist. In troughs of clarity between waves of numbing infusions, the coder broods on his brood. No dullards, his son and daughter. They will have to confront the oddball contortions of their father, whose drug-fogged brain pulses to the metronomic, digitized equipage recording his vitals. Dual inarguables: the parrot killed him, and he failed to kill the parrot simultaneously. The police therefore scraped from the roadway only a shell. The envoy it housed? Recalled to the molecule and its executives, perhaps already meting abuse on a different infringer. Steep downside also to his accidental revival. Had his termination lasted, much that might have settled now roils once again.

The status of his penance. The completion-state of his punishment. The likelihood of retribution redux, vendetta for his unsuccessful revenge. As time ferries him gradually away from pain, his mind gropes toward its established restlessness. An unremitting churning. Within his skull: the wincing plasm. He takes his wife's advice, hides from the professionals an explication of the parrot, but can't reprise a man who simply made a stupid decision. Contents himself with obedience. He speaks only when he must advertise his docility and amiability. His first-order task? To obviate his constraints. Takes him a long period. Aided in this quest by his recovery requirements. His physical therapists direct him under conditions of free-movement. He displays an easygoing, trustworthy attitude. Less straightforward to manifest a mental parallel. The resident alienists, informed of his history, won't hoodwink. They confer with his psychologist and blockade the avenue of dissimulation. Silence combined with waiting: his only viable strategy. The coder ripens into a mute. He believes his cunning will prove fruitful. In a room large enough for pacing and thinking, he resigns himself to time. Indomitable, ever-renewable, indifferent time. Days, months, weeks, years: isotropes. Time also cyclic, paganly unteleological as it replenishes itself in the instant of its expiration. The coder's body: his clock and transport, eventually sans restraints in a discreet penetralium. Alone but for the visits of professionals and family members. Extending from a high corner of the garret: the de-orbited eye of a television he never activates. Its barren surface conjures his screen-spent days. Stillness now. Serenity in staring. At the wall. Out the window. Into the middle distance. His greatest challenge? Quiescence before his family. Confounding to him, their myriad and well-founded alterations of "Why?" Done with lying. Enough damage. Enough pain. The fallout has powdered everyone with a fine coating of toxic grit. When he thinks of a decontamination procedure, he will speak. Until then, mum. He has given up on the veridical as a cleanser of universal application. The truth makes sense only to him, or makes *something* to him related to sense. His actions, the months of slow buildup and the acute final day, resulted from biological states. He obeyed his emotions and thoughts, behaved in accordance with his specs. How to articulate this? He could fumfer in grunts, but that would only nettle his family twofold, since his mono and disyllables would come across as unintelligible. The healing of his body does not shake his resolve. And his wife, disheartened upon one of her visits, slaps him. Children in attendance. Witnesses as shocked as he. Aflame, the left side of his face. Neck wrenched from the power of the blow. Anti-regretful, his wife's comportment. Her hand described a pugilist's arc. From her lower body flowed her walloping power. She positioned her feet. She aligned her hips. She followed through. No remorse. The coder perceives in her ending posture the energy she has stockpiled. Perceives also her desire to have hit him harder and more often and with a closed fist. She straightens, dangles her hand. Relieving it of pain? Limbering it for another roundhouse? "Mom." His daughter, with his son's frightened eyes reinforcing her. The coder's wife? Dissuaded, but not without disgust. Common reaction to the moral choice. He himself has felt it many times. De-escalate. Someone must. Woozy, he sits down by the window. The human-side originator of all this strife, the locus of chaos, turned peacemaker. Others have achieved metanoia. Now so shall he. Withholds active resistance. Passive only. "Dad, are you all right?" His son. "Of course he's all right. I didn't hit him that hard." "Not that hard? I think you gave him whiplash." His daughter. He holds up a hand. Mute, not cataleptic. His children: protective even after everything he has put them through. His love for them all but melts him to the floor. He goes to his son and daughter, holds them in one embrace, wishes to include his wife, but she steps away. He encircles his children until he feels their discomfort. Natural. Retreats. His vow must hold. Until? Again, an estimate fails to alight. Disquiet sends his eyes to the floor, one hand to his chin, the other to his head, where he scratches and scratches. He must claw out the larval answer just beneath his scalp. His nails rasp and dig. His wife extends an arm, sweeps the children behind her. The coder rearranges himself. Knows the impression he has made. Clasps his hands behind his back. Professorial. Must look out the window, not at his family. His wife ushers herself and the children into the hallway, closes the door with the gentlest thrust of the latch into the jamb. As if not to disturb him. As if he sleeps. Beyond the window: deciduous trees. Maples, the only ones he can identify. Of the parking spaces visible, many more filled than empty. Big business, healthcare in the homeland. Don't cure. Treat. The most mellifluous word known to Aesculapians? Chronic, which translates to perpetual revenue. Outside the door, his wife consults with the latest professionals. His psychologist, persona non grata. Passed beyond her ken, his case. He wants to crack the aperture and peep upon those who'll captain his future. The impetuous, non-starter option: tear the door open and scram. He wouldn't reach the end of the block. Security would corral him, club him into repose, drag him back here, his dwelling place for the present and future of indeterminate duration. Where his psyche quakes. Let it, but within a quiet, compliant body. No reason in that case for pharmaceutical damping into more pleasing seismography. Return home? Perambulate unsupervised? Too much to hope for. He has overstressed society's tolerances. Irrefragably harmless to the commonweal, he has still and all shown himself unfit for sovereign personal recognizance. His wife hires a zealous advocate who wrests a limited victory from the controlling legal authorities: indefinite custodial care with periodic evaluations. The coder in court, as unobtrusive as the coder in his room. And the judgment doubtless urged into actuality by his ability to subvent his own confinement. If only every hearing ended with the state not appropriating a boarder. His transfer thereafter to another facility. Another room with different windows giving onto verdant grounds. Staff emphasize the privacy of his accommodations, encourage him to develop a sense of ownership. The four walls? Diabase-filled gabions, his palms detect when he splays them on the plaster. His door, not locked from the outside. He can't lock it from the inside. His behavior alone drives the protocol. Could go from unlocked to locked. To sealed shut and alarmed. To him locked within and locked down. He won't squander forbearance. His ankle bracelet saves him from thoughts of escape. All in all, a comfortable and soothing habitat. Others will answer whether permanent. His enterprise? To occupy time and render it not-wasted, since he possesses it now in quantities limited perhaps only by his lifespan. Staff propose stimuli. Books? His mind at present too manic for reading. Television? Don't make him weep. The arts? Wouldn't know which end of a brush to hold. He indicates the pen in staff's breast pocket. "My foul-up. Should have left it at home. Could be used as a weapon." Staff, removing the pen and sealing it in a drawer. "If you want to write or sketch, look in the art materials. There are pastels, charcoal sticks, some chalk. Couldn't stab jelly with any of them. That's why they're okay. Feel free. Here's paper." The coder chooses a black pastel and sits at a large table in the common area. Writes nothing. Places the pastel atop the paper. Considers the pairing. The day-one analog version of the journal he began at the psychologist's instigation. That document: at home on his computer. As good as combusted. Begin again. The idea intrigues him. He remembers enough to start through repetition. Not explain, less justify. More narrate, describe. If he cannot move those who despise him into forgiveness, he can at least try to provide thorough context for their disdain. He will consume time in abundance, maybe even profit by the reserves at his disposal. Allocution. All lives should come to it. Now his has. He devotes himself to a hypergraphia of thick-lined, crumbly scrawl. Staff inspects all he produces, finds in his output nothing harmful nor minatory, hands the pages back to him to stack on a steadily rising ream. When obliging him for interchange, staff prompts him to write. "We know you can do it. You do it all day. Why waste time with gestures and facial expressions?" Risking demerits, he perdures with manual semaphore. What he writes: not for staff. For circles of the elect. Staff humors him. His days pass in scribbling, peering, eating without tasting. He sleeps on linens changed daily. Obeys the demands of his body in a bathroom cleaned weekly. Content to wear copies of the same clothes, day upon day. Visits and visitors peter. The coder understands diminishing returns, how the rational identifies a sunk cost and jabs it toward the margins. Troubles him, that his family will have to claim him as a deduction. His work distracts him from what he cannot control. The trees outside green and pale, flourish and wither. Wetness and brightness and dryness and mudness and darkness and frostness betide in their turns the land. Up and down in concert, the exterior temperature. His room and the building? Climate-controlled between sixty-eight and seventy-two degrees year-round. The sun and moon exchange places. Thousands of shiftings as he generates and organizes his harvest. Someday, his family might delve. In the present, he holds to his task, gimlet-eyed always for a hint of scarlet through the panes, and as he progresses, he finds himself yearning agog for a tarriance. If he cannot seek it with catabasis, perhaps it will deign to ascend. Hearken, psychopomp. His aphonic request for a peaceful conclave. No one else, no *thing* else, can appreciate his insights. He has looked hard at the midst. He has treasured his filched embers and deployed them for light. Thus his paramount crime: wrongheaded use. Obvious now. Caliginous throughout. He should have called down the wind, the gale, the simoom. Should have nurtured white heat, cast it about, not for comfort nor warmth nor least to create, but to lick where it will, perhaps all the Earth over. And burn.